Abby Maria Hemenway

The Mystical Rose

Abby Maria Hemenway

The Mystical Rose

ISBN/EAN: 9783337370695

Printed in Europe, USA, Canada, Australia, Japan

Cover: Foto ©Andreas Hilbeck / pixelio.de

More available books at **www.hansebooks.com**

THE

MYSTICAL ROSE;

OR,

Mary of Nazareth,

The Lily of the House of David.

I AM THE ROSE OF SHARON AND THE LILY OF THE VALLEY.—CANTICLES.
MANY DAUGHTERS HAVE DONE VIRTUOUSLY, BUT THOU EXCELLEST THEM ALL.—SOLOMON.
BLESSED ART THOU AMONG WOMEN.—GABRIEL.

BY

MARIÈ JOSEPHINE.

NEW YORK:

D. APPLETON AND COMPANY.

1865.

To

Mary of Heaven.

Rosa Mystica.

" O, 'tis a blessed privilege of ours
   To thread the Paradise of Heavenly flowers,
   And gaze upon the fairest rose." . . . .
" O, may the dew which sparkles on thy stem,
   Be gently shaken from thy diadem
   And earthly bound, drop softly from thy bower.'

    .   .   .   .

" And may my heart be opened to receive,"
   . . . . " and with joy perceive"
  . . " flowers rising to the view,
   Watered within me by that Heavenly dew."

The Lily of the House of David.

"Seest thou that diadem bending low,
  As if modestly shunning its beauty to show?
  Look at those petals of silvery white,
  Girt round with a halo."   .   .   .   .

" That lily is lovely, but lovelier still
  Was the flower that blossomed on Bethlehem's hill;
  And white as the snow as its petals are,
  That Virgin of virgins was fairer far."

PREFATORY.

Books I., II., and III. were written, and V. and VI. in part, before we had seen any traditional Life of the Virgin. We supposed ourself almost alone upon the ground. The rich poems of Willis, *David's Child* and *Jephtha's Fair Daughter*, walked not too near the One radiant Rose. Ingraham's *Prince of the House of David* came. The brilliant pen had left still untraced the Lily of the House. Was it an ambition, the charm of a subject untouched,* or the attraction of a few olden pictures (paintings of Luke,† Matthew, and John, growing as studied " like a transparency illuminated, behind which the light necessary for its development shining, it comes out" ever more and more beautiful) stirred the untried pen? Fearlessly we took up the subject at first. Was it divining it given, tranquilly expectant of the gift by little and little, in faith with its inherent virtue to supply and outshine of itself? In the

---

* We had not read till we were at press the eloquent little book, *Pictures of the Virgin and her Son*, by Rev. Charles Beecher.

† According to tradition, Luke was an artist, and painted a portrait of Christ and the Blessed Virgin, copies of which, *some* piously think, may perhaps have been handed down to this day, or at least to the days of the great artists who designed the Christ-heads and Madonnas.

quiet of Sabbaths it grew, in the calm before the ringing of bells, in the hush of holy eves. It was hopefully, enjoyedly written ; till, threading at length the catacombs of tradition, lost in a labyrinth of beauty, pious allegory, ancient and mystic, luminous legend, livingly warm with words that burn, shedding odors as incense from a censer, we were overwhelmed. How little had we said ! How little could we say with the already said ! "The Queen loveth judgment," who can praise her beauty ? Never felt we incompleteness as in this: and yet, little book, in thy poor finiteness thou mayest bear to some souls the sweet hint " the beauty of Jesus is inexhaustible." Thou art written, and no more ours. Go forth and tell in the garden of Mary every breeze sighs of Him whom to know is life and love. " Every tree, every flower, the very turf smells of Jesus." Bid another come and see.

ACKNOWLEDGMENTS.

The Holy Family belong to the world, we took as our motto, and have appropriated every coveted relic or tradition handed down by historian, Christian or pagan, from the archives of Latin Church, Hebrew, or Greek, coming within scope of our original plan, only careful to note wherever a tradition has been thus introduced. We have, moreover, availed ourself of the note-references of others to a limited extent ; and least may forget, while we spare their names " crucifixion in a preface," to record the indebtedness we are under to several Christian and scholarly friends who have rendered valuable assistance in our research for traditional lore.

LUDLOW, VT., 7th October, 1864.

BOOKS.

BOOK I.

OR

Book of the Mysteries.

" Christ hath sent us down the angels,
      And the whole earth and the skies
    Are illumed by altar-candles
      Lit for blessed mysteries;
    And a Priest's hand through creation,
    Waveth calm and consecration.

" Truth is fair—should we forego it?
      Can we sigh right for a wrong?
    God Himself is the best Poet.
    *   *   *   *
" Sing His truth out fair and full,
      And secure His beautiful."

                              Mrs. Browning.

CONTENTS.

Rosa Mystica.

CHAPTER I.

INVOCATION.

O FOR the morning dew and wine of song!
O for the psalm from God!

                    Thou, who didst wear
Our nature like a vesture pure, and hang
It on the rood of Calvary 'tween God
And man, this pregnant brain upon, Christ-priest,
O, gently lay the consecrating hand!

Thrice blessèd touch!   A mystery infinite
Unrolls.   The Father from His throne o'erleans,
T' drop His smile upon th' Babe on Mary's breast,
And all the angels sing.   Soft falls on head

And heart the anointing reverence rich :
I thank Thee, God!   Amen! Amen!

                     And Thou,—
If sainted spirit may gaze down on earth,
The glorified ones walk our mortal turf,—
Sweet Mary, from the shining windows bright,
Within thy heavenly mansion, lean in sight,
Its golden threshold cross, stand at the pearly gate,—
Sweet Mother of the Christ, one glimpse I wait!

A brightness trembles down the hearkening skies,
I catch the glory of her loving eyes!
Thanks! thanks! O, Angel-maid, for sweetest theme
That ever tranced a soul in sacred dream,
Bright Mother-maid! bright Babe, incarnate born,
The Rose on Judah's stript and withered thorn!

O, golden Rose of Paradise encrowned!
O, Mother of the sceptred Prince enthroned!
All beauty-floodings of earth, air, or sea,
Poured o'er my soul, I offer thee,
And lay my song-heart panting at thy feet.
Outspread thy hands in benediction sweet,—
(So that some other morn when I may stand
In Heaven, I may not blush to hold the leaves

Of my poor book before thy shining face:)
Vouchsafe this grace, this love, this favor me,
Be with my spirit while I sing of thee!

Amen.

Sweet gift of inspiration high
Glow like the ancient star and light the way.

CHAPTER II.

PART I.

EXPECTANCY.

WE journey back to the Past, back to the Hebrew days and Palestine, before the Rod of Jesse had blossomed, or a prophet had sung, "And thou, Bethlehem, in the land of Judah,"—"before Moses was,"—"before Abraham was,"—to the days of expectancy and Eden.

"I WILL PUT ENMITY BETWEEN THEE AND THE WOMAN, AND BETWEEN THY SEED AND HER SEED: IT SHALL BRUISE THY HEAD."

THE apple stain fresh on her lip,
  Her shamed eye growing to the turf,
Yet still these mystic words took root
In woman's heart, first, last, fruitful

Of sweet belief in all things high,
Or fond,—nor all the after curse
Could wipe it out,—"SHALL BRUISE THY HEAD."

Eve rocked her babe, and thought—"*perhaps!*"—
Old Noah's wife above the drownèd earth,
Looked on her *three*, and questioned—"*which?*"
Great Babel's smitten neighborhood,
Each from his stammering brother turned,
And yet, expectancy in gleams
Through all the shivered nation ran:
Here, Egypt's Isis zodiacal;
There, Sching-mu,[1] goddess-woman's seed;
Here, Thibet's god[2] of virgin-birth;
Where India's spice-groves drug the air,
Budha of Maiha-maiha born;
And Somonokodon, the prince
And god, the Sun with Siam's maid
Enamored, kissed with rays that gave;
And Lao Tseu from earth-nymph sprung
"As jasper wondrous beautiful,"
And Chrichna in a grotto swathed,
While angels sing and shepherds come—
And Zoroaster,[3] the magi seer,
Snatched from the tyrant Nemroud's sword;
And Paraguay's wild copper tribes,

EXPECTANCY.

Where burn the mountains of the sun,
With god incarnate, working well
The miracles that fix the seal,
Transfigured to a burning sun,
All, chastely sprung of peerless maids;
Symbol and count expectancy:

But dim the light on barbarous shrines
That shimmers but in broken gleams,
To the rich glow magnificent,
Where faithful Abram's princely tent,
On Mamre's plain, transfigured stands.
His seed, like stars, the patriarch counts,
And princess Sarah laughs for joy,
And, woman like, believing more
Than woman's cautious lips confess,
Wins fresh her waning beauty back,
Her woman-youth, her woman-love,
And clasps the heir of faith and heaven;
Or over him, exiled and worn,
Who pillowed on the Bethel stone
And saw the ladder reach to heaven,
And in his dying vision-rapt
The Shiloh where the sceptre fades.
Thence down the bright Messiac chain,
Till unsurpassed Isaiah sings,

1*

And Israel's sweetest psalmist chants
The birth as pure as morning dew.
But David dies, and prophesy
Is dumb, not dead, her words all spoke,
And reverent waiting—but for God.

PART II.

TRADITION.

As the expectancy of God's people was slowly, but fully culminating, not far from Mount Carmel lived a poor woman, a widow, whose name was Anna, of the tribe of Levi.[4] Her husband, not long dead, was from the tribe of Juda and family of David, a just man, whose name was Joachim;[5] and who had loved his wife so tenderly and well, the fathers record, while the great Hebrew stigma, a childless wedlock, caused them to go sorrowing, he still clave with a beautiful affection to the spouse of his youth. And, indeed, from these same grave fathers it appears that Anna was one of those women of tender and exalted virtues, from whom no worthy man, having shared the rich intimacy of their devotion, could turn aside. Thus when the hope of offspring had died, leaving them saddened, yet kindly affectioned, as in the days of their espousal, this godly twain walked "blameless in life." And "God visited them," and God gave them—"a son?" No. "Had Joachim, had Anna hoped for one?" But God gave them gift special, gift direct, and God ever knoweth the gift he giveth his beloved. Mary of Nazareth, the incomparable daughter, was born, in the year of Rome 734, September 8th;[6] and Anna, rejoicing at her birth, this canticle sang:

" Cantabo laudem Domino meo, quia visitavit me et abstulit a me opprobrium amicorum meorum. Et dedit mihi fructum justitiæ mul-

tiplicem in conspectu tuo. Quis amicorum audite ! audite ! Filii Reuben quod Anna lactat! Audite ! Audite duodecim tribus Israel, quia Anna lactat.".... [7]

CHAPTER III.

THE WIDOW OF NAZARETH.

" How sweet the breath beneath the hill
Of Sharon's dewy rose!"

WITHIN a cottage thatched with moss,
O'er which twin palms their green arms cross
As if in prayer;
Where the lattice-bars are bright with bloom,
And the rose-breath scents the rustic room,
A mother in Israel, mellowed and fair,
Though the waves of silver ripple her hair,
Though the robe of the widow-cloth sobers her form,
Smiles as the bow o'er the grave of the storm.

The wheel of spinning by her side,
The distaff in her hand,
She draws with skill the flaxen thread,
Our matron-mother bland.

The circling spokes sing round,
　　The busy fliers whirr,
　　The spinner's lips just stir
In harmony of sound.

　　The moments come, the moments go,
The hours of the morn in their freshness wane,
The hours of the noon march in again,
　　Our aged spinner spinneth slow,
Till the hand forgetting its cunning skill,
The active wheel is a-dream and still;
And where is our weary spinner now,
The dreamer with fair and placid brow?

Adrift in the sweet siesta lost:
　　Gray thought glints back to damsel-days,
　　To a life as fresh as forest-lays,
The bridges of the past are crossed—
Crossed till the aged spinner wins
Her lily maidhood back;
Crossed till the fair betrothed again
Her golden bridehood clasps,
And wears the rose of love in flower;
Or kisses with delicious love,
Love's crowning gift, the artless dove

That coos and nestles to its rest
Within the happy mother-breast;
And years roll on with sheaves of joy,
Till on their retrospective track
The years of bliss have all crept back,
And sighing sweep from off the track,
Where roll the sadder memories back;
Till glooms the ghast and sable bier,
And lost love drops the tribute tear;
Yet brightly all the thinking while,
She seems to keep this thought and smile :
While I from bitter springs may drink,
This earth has still one golden link,
One rose aneath the cypress tree,
One rose that sweetly blooms for me,
One love that beautifies the earth,
One love that warms the widowed hearth.

Half Asleep.

Dreamily, dreamily, the burning moments of the Syrian noon
drop among the sands of Time! The golden heap growing one
sand higher, one sand deeper, growing till the glass is turned—till
the invisible glass is turned! And the matron arouses and looks
through the lattice, yet clogged with her dream—looks through the
lattice into a garden—a quiet garden near, where the hillside northward dips—dips down unto, or looms up against—over and against,
and shuts in like a wall, like the wise son of Sirach's beloved, a
garden enclosed—a quiet garden enclosed, where the rill that glides

from the hillside in warbles as a nightingale half asleep—half asleep —through the flowery nooks and borders.   In the midst of the gar- den, Mary of Nazareth walks—walks under the trees—walks amid the thyme and roses—walks beside the quiet rill in the quiet garden —walks—and the mother watches the maiden walk. Blessed Anna- mother !

ANNA

(*Watching the maiden walking under the trees*).

Now bent caressingly
   O'er some sweet bud unfolding,
Sweetness less than thee,
   Its nectared petals holding.
O brightly now, and ever thus thy fair self seems,
Like the angels we see in a vision of dreams.

   From the green to the blue,
     From the earth to the sky
   Uprises thy glance
     From a praise-lit eye,
As though thou wouldst look into heaven ;
     As pure as the breath
     From the lip of the thyme,
     As pure as the dew
     From the heart of the rose,
Each breath but a prayer to the Holy given.
O, the crown of our love, the heaven hath he,
Thy father hath heaven, but I have thee !

O the joy of my heart and the joy of my eyes!
Look down! look down!   The angels may bear thee away
   to the skies!

How will this heart grow lone
   When I shall miss
      Thy step so light,
   And pure love-kiss
      At morn and night;
Aye, feel itself alone!

Ah, thy betrothed too soon will come,
   To claim my love, my pride,
And I must yield my treasure up
   And give with smile his bride.

O, ever thus the mother-lot,
   Her smiles how rimmed with tears,
To see another hand ingrasp
   The flower she fondest rears!

Nor would I wish it otherwise,
   To be beloved is woman's dower;
And sacred are the social ties
   That o'er her heart have power.

And thou wilt make thy home
A precious spot, I know,
Where grasses green will grow,
And love-flowers bud and blow,
And sweet the hope-birds sing,
And weave their fruitful nest
Amid the clustering leaves,
Aneath thy cottage eaves.

And thy betrothed, I look on him
With honest Hebrew pride,
He was thy father's friend and kin,[8]
'Tis meet thou be his bride.

A carpenter in humble guise,
In line of David's throne,
A bridegroom-prince were Judah not
A slave to heathen Rome.

And thou, my Mary, modest maid,
Sprung of the royal race,
In thy rich veins the blood of kings
Flows with a charmèd grace.

But I must haste my task :
Or e'er thy robe I've spun,

Or veil of bridal wrought,
    For his betrothed he'll ask ;
And I should blush to say,
    Delay the nuptial-feast,
Defer the marriage-day.

———+———

CHAPTER IV.

THE COMMISSION.

"THE ANGEL GABRIEL WAS SENT FROM GOD."—LUKE I. 26.

GOD spake !————————————————————
   The choralists of heaven, cherub and harp,
Mirrored in columns on the crystal floor ;
Nor breath, nor rustle of an angel's wing
Stirred on the vast profound.   The minstrel breeze—
The river of the Throne—stayed its bright flow ;
And heaven was still. God spake: through radiant
    ranks
Of seraphim transfixed, the uttered Voice
Rolled like the sound of many waters' call,
And he who stood archangel there bowed till
His bright brow touched the footstool all a-glow.

CHAPTER V.

ANNUNCIATION.

"AND THE ANGEL CAME."—LUKE I. 28-38.

> " O'er the wave of Galilee
>   Hark, what sounds of wonder sweep,
>   Strange, unearthly, sweet, yet deep,
>   Though in their intensity
>   None might word or symbol know,
>   Who upon its margin trod,
>   Save ono maid like purest snow—"

DOWN in a little garden-grotto where
  Gray jutting rock and tree and floweret fair,
        The quaintest alcove form,
Where deftly o'er the velvet mosses strewn,
The rich pomegranate's scarlet blossoms sown
        The fragrant turf adorn,

Where gradual slopes the banklet drapery bright
Down to a rill that glides from sound and sight,
        Beneath the cypress shade,
Unwistful of the silent flow of time,
Lost in the vista of a revery sublime,
        Reclines a soul-rapt maid,

Whose steadfast eye doth o'er a parchment run,
An heirloom treasured down from sire to son,
      A blurred and ancient scroll.
Her rosy fingers its worn columns trace,
A heaven-dropped truth illumes her modest face,
      She bends anear the roll;

Her rich eye melts, her heart responsive thrills,
The bright'ning meditation all her spirit fills,
      And fans each ardent breath;
O Father, when, All-Glorious Father, will
The Swift Deliverer come, this to fulfil,
      And save from sin and death?

O Israel's God! Thy Zion waits her King;
When will this Peace-Prince her salvation bring?
      Thy word of promise gleams
Here on this scriptured page, prophetic bright,
As through these fair boughs slants the quivering light
      Of sunset's parting beams.

And lo, now brightened on each blessed word
The amber twilight glistens as though stirred
      With fresh-shed altar-fire,
O seraph brought! O visioned glowing coal,
That fed and fanned with zeal the flaming soul
      And lips of rapt Isaiah!

O, happy Virgin thou, whose maiden arm
Shall cradle the young Prince of Peace, and charm
            His eyelids bright to sleep,
His loveliest of lovely heads to rest
In blissful slumbers on thy hallowed breast.
          ` O heavenliest charge to keep !

Thy bosom shelter give to Jesse's fair
And Budding Rod—to Jesse's Royal Heir,
           O, gift beyond compare !
Whence sheds this deep delightful awe ?
A charm on evening's brow I never saw,
           Mirrors in earth and air.

On this gray knoll where lingering verdures creep,
Th' honeyed violets that through each crevice peep
           Seem each an incense-cup
O'erbrimmed with purest incense sent,
Fragrant and sweet, to the great heavens o'erbent,
           Offered in silence up.

Each reverent leaf on rose and cypress round
Stands stirless in the calm. The gush of sound
           Forgets yon pulsing rill,
A conscious hush on every brightened wave ;
A mystic beauty twilight never gave
           The sky and landscape fill,

The soft air purer grows, and odorous now
The atmosphere floods with celestial glow ;
        My veil aside be found,
My sandals, be ye loosed from off my feet,
Wait, soul, the vision of the Lord to meet.
        This place is holy ground.

Her meek head bows—her warm lips press the scroll
Close-clasped unto the heart that 'gainst it beats
With awe expectant grown—nor looks she up
Until her drooped eye gathers glow of heaven,
And Gabriel before her stands—the light
From his resplendent wings brightening the turf
Unto her feet—inclined his radiant brow.
. . . . " And all the earth appeared to stand
        In the great overflow
Of light celestial from his wings and head."
A speechless awe through her fear-parted lips
Half breathes, and from her wonder-drinking eyes
Looks trembling out.   The glory half in smile,
The reverent angel veils.

GABRIEL.

Ave, Maria,
Gracia plena ! (or, Mary full of grace,
Sweet hail!) Hail, Virgin honored of the Lord !

Fear not; for thou with God hast favor found;
With Him the cherubims amid, who sits.
The friendship of the Lord is thine;
Of thee Messiah shall be born.   Fear not!

The meek maid feels the revelation clasp
And hold her soul astonished great;
Yet there is kindness large, and triumph high,
The angelic greeting in, that lifts unto the plain
Of trust, and nerves the lips that pondering stir
With the low-questioned how?   "How can it be?"
The tall bright angel looketh kindly down
Upon the maiden at his feet (for she
Is blessed of the Lord, nor faithless drifts;
'Tis but an anchor cast out for the " how,"
The human looking up to God).

GABRIEL.

The glory of the Lord shall shadow thee.

MARY.

The handmaid of the Lord behold!   Amen!

CHAPTER VI.

ANNUNCIATION NIGHT.

Scene—*Ten o'clock, in Mary's Chamber.*

"I LANGUISH WITH LOVE, HIS LEFT HAND IS UNDER MY HEAD AND HIS RIGHT HAND SHALL EMBRACE ME."—CANTICLES ii. 5-6.

IN through every lattice-bar
Where the trellis gapes ajar,
Flowing in, golden bright,
Beams of Paridisial light,
With a wondrous " lily-bloom,"
Flooding all the blessed room,
Silver most the snowy cover
Draping light the sleeper over.

Hush! a footfall on the floor;
Human step at chamber door.
Now with eye of wonder mild,
Bending o'er her radiant child,
Gazing long doth Anna ponder,
Till her loosed lips breathe the wonder.

ANNA.

'Never saw I moonbeams bright
As around this couch to-night
Gleaming o'er thy forehead fair
Glistening in thy lustrous hair ;
What a shining arrow dips
In the smile around thy lips !'
(Bows her head to kiss the sleeper.)
'O, Great Father, safely keep her!
(Saying, turning from the door,)
' 'Tis a vision, nothing more.
'Tis a sweet and mystic dreaming—
Nights are never all in seeming.'
(Leaves her to her radiant rest
Guarded by an angel-guest.)

CHAPTER VII.

THE VISITATION.

PART I.

"THE WINTER IS PAST, THE RAIN IS OVER AND GONE; THE FLOWERS APPEAR ON THE EARTH; THE TIME OF THE SINGING OF BIRDS IS COME, AND THE VOICE OF THE TURTLE IS HEARD IN OUR LAND. RISE UP, MY LOVE, MY FAIR ONE, AND COME AWAY."—SOL. SONG.

"AND MARY AROSE UP IN THOSE DAYS, AND WENT INTO THE HILL COUNTRY WITH HASTE."—LUKE I. 39–56.

WHERE, like nest in mountain pine,
 Crowned with cedar, girt with thyme,
Of the world, and yet apart,
Hebron city drew her heart.

Tradition writes she rode a white mule, named Elabathonia; but unto us—with the first consciousness of the bright coming motherhood surging through all her glorified being, free from taste of weariness, or taint of pain—she comes through the narrow plain, going up with footsteps as an angel, "the country on every side overhung with mountains."

To her lightly sandalled foot
Cushioned seemed each grassy root;
O'er her head the heavens blue
Lovingly bent down to view;

E'en the hotly panting sun
Seemed her favored brow to shun,
While he showered his golden rain,
Deftly o'er the flowery plain,
Sun and shine her pathway round
Touched not Mary, but the ground.[10]

Taking from sweet choice the paths most retired, entering now upon the wild ravine, going up now the solitary way

Through the flowery fell and wood
Where the partridge leads her brood;

where the hart, "panting for the water-brooks," comes to drink; where the wild goats all day browse, and the young kids at play go up and down the flower-wreathed cliffs, and the timid "pigeons, with their rich wings settling on the rocks," brood in flocks at the noonday. Beautiful young daughter of David, "all thy garments smell of myrrh, aloes, and cassia." "Beautiful are thy feet among the mountains."

PART II.

Tiled with brown and trellised white,
Zachary's mansion looms in sight:
Through the porch and at the door,
Brightening in her gladness more,
With a voice so filled with Heaven
Is her salutation given,

And such high celestial grace
Beams upon her lighted face,
Elizabeth with transport sees,
And trembles in the Heavenly breeze ;
All her being swayed and stirred
As outpours the spirit word :
" Blessed of the Lord and Heaven,
Unto thee is welcome given ;
Soon with babe upon thy breast,
O'er all women thou'lt be blest.
Wherefore am I honored so ?
Why should I such favor know ?
Wherefore, mother of my Lord,
Come to me with first accord ?
What a heaven my spirit filled,
What a love my heart enthrilled,
Soon as e'er thy voice I heard,
Grace-endowed, my unborn stirred,
Leaped for joy at hail of thine,
Waits with love the word divine.'

Light is in the Virgin's eye,
Light enkindled from the sky,
Glowings from her rapt lips start,
Glowings fresh from Heaven and heart.

That sublime, sudden outpouring of the

M A G N I F I C A T.

My soul doth magnify the Lord, and my spirit is ravished with joy in God my Saviour.

Because he hath regarded the humility of his handmaid; for behold, from henceforth I shall be called blessed during the course of all ages.   Because he who is mighty hath done great things in me, and holy is his name.

And his mercy is from generation to generation to them that fear him.

He hath showed might in his arm; he hath scattered the proud in the conceit of their hearts.

He hath pulled down the mighty from their throne, and hath exalted the humble.

He hath filled the hungry with good things, and the rich he hath sent empty away.

He hath been mindful of his mercy, and hath taken Israel his servant under his protection.

According to the promise which he hath made to our fathers, Abraham, and to his seed forever.

And the hymn the Virgin sings

Down through all the ages rings.

Written upon the leaves of every Bible, it lives "the principal canticle of the New Testament."

PART III.

THREE MONTHS.

Now the residence [11] of Zacharias was situated at the rich bottom of one of those fertile valleys that abound in the hill country of Judea; and in its rear extended one of those gardens called *Paradise* among the Persians; where grew every fair tree of Palestine and fragrant exotics transplanted from *Nilus* and Araby the Happy, or the far Euphrates: the alma tree crowning its fruit with its purple blooms; the crimsoned-blossomed coral tree outshining "the knots of flowers carelessly spread along in the glades;" and streams fed from the fountain of the court glided silently away under the groups of orange trees filling the air with their delicious perfumes; and the place was all beautiful, for

> Priest Zachary, he was rich,
> High priest—one of the sacred twenty-four; [12]
> Renowned and fair his ancient house and court;
> Yet with simplicity—like good men's homes
> And ancient days—simplicity withal.

Here this "spotless dove of beauty" folded her wing in sweet security. This gifted and poetic daughter of Israel's poet-kings contemplated at holy leisure in the near distance the vast expanding sea whose billows washed the echoing Syrian shore, or the deep sounding forest of cedars around, till her prophetic lips trembled in rapturous murmur: "He cometh; then shall all the trees of the wood rejoice;" or bent in pensive admiration over the lilies of the valley that grew at her feet—the rich lilies to which she is likened by Solomon in his mystical canticle; and gathered and cherished a thought of the minute care: "They toil not, neither do they spin;" and linked with the tender love of the beautiful and the lowly, the poems of a brown earth blowing out among the grasses of the field, the flowers, suggestive flowers, is this tradition the Persians still keep: "One day the glorious Virgin Mary laid her hand on the stem of a flower, called by the Arabs Arthenita (we call it sweet cyclamen), when by the touch of her hand was communicated to the plant a delicious fragrance it has since retained." And the Christians of the East point out a spring in the mountains to which she frequently directed her steps, and which bears to-day the name of Mary. "And she abode with Elizabeth for the space of three months." In the garden of Zachary, in this "garden of delights," walked Mary and Elizabeth; arm in arm walked Mary and Elizabeth. Elizabeth soon to be a mother of a son to be a prophet, and more than a prophet, and Mary, whom the fathers have euphoniously named "the Flower of the Earth," pondering in loveliest humility, silently, but raptly, the angelic annunciation, "Son of the Highest."

And Zachary? Zachary in those days was dumb,
And wonderingly looked on the blessed two.

PART IV.

Three months had flown,
Like days in Paradise, where God's elect
Transparent walk, as one continuous day
Of brightness lapsed; and they who would not lose
One minute-moment of commune so sweet,
The world's two women sit by Zachary's well,

Beside the well, or fountain in the court,
Where seven tall lemons stood in flower around,
With seats beneath for lord or guest.   The place
I've said was fair.   The hour ? the early night.
A dreamy, rich, delicious Judean night.
From thicket aromatic, tender comes
The warble of the thrush that sweetest sings
At dewy eve.   Glow-worms the grasses light,
The baya's [13] nest illumes her tree,
And " nightingales, whose hearts leap as they sing
Unto the moon," the rose-woods thrill ;
                    But I—
Within this garden—looked to see
The world's two women close by Zachary's well.
One, rich in much experience and years,
Blameless in life, and lovelier with age ;
The constant silver light upon her chastened face,
Growing each blessed day more saintly bright—
A woman who grows never old but ripe,—
Nor meeker matron in the land, she sits
Meek by the well, the great prayer of her life
Almost fulfilled ; yet with a woman's dread,
Her lawful dread, looming like a soft cloud
Of sadness in her eyes to-night.   And one,
The maid of Nazareth, the moon that cast
Its floodings on the floodings of her hair,

Of brown the goldenest, less beautiful.
But we have now upon a beauty touched,
A beauty [14] more than words.

                         The holy night
Is over them; of holy things they talk,
And reverently radiant hopes that rise
Born of the wondrous prophecies of old;
She whose rich voice is softly sad to night,
And she, with lips intoned with heaven and love,
That sovereign love that over human souls
Holds charm and calm.   O woman-sympathy,
So priceless precious in its preciousnesss.
Sweet women of the Testament of grace,
We leave ye to your cup of mystery and love,
Ye visited of God.

—◆—

NOTES TO BOOK I.

1. Sching-mu, " son of one of the most popular Chinese goddesses, begotten by the touch of a water flower, and brought up in the hut of a fisherman, who became an illustrious personage and worker o. miracles."

2. The god Fo, worshipped in China and in a part of the eastern peninsula of India, born of Llamoghiuprul, the beautiful betrothed of a king, alike remarkable for the beauty of her person and sanctity of life.

3. " The Babylonian Dogdo sees in a dream," runs this Eastern myth, " a messenger from Oramazes, resplendent with light, laying at her feet superb garments; a celestial ray falls on the countenance of the sleeper, and she becomes as beautiful as the day star.   Zer-

duscht Zoraster, or rather Ebraïm-Zer-Ateucht, the celebrated prophet of the magi, is the fruit of this nocturnal vision. The tyrant Nemroud, informed by his astrologers that a child about being born threatened destruction to his gods and his throne, put to the sword every woman in his dominion who was thought to be pregnant."

4. *Vide* " The Unanimity of the Evangelists."

5. Joachim signified " Preparation of the Lord," or, according to Galitinus, " God raises and confirms." The names Joachim and Anna are indeed mystic, and historians question whether they are real or but mystical names of the church. The Bollandists, Serri, and other writers rank them as mystical, but the torrent of theologians and critics hold the contrary. *Vide* Trombelli, *Life of St. Joachim and St. Anna;* Tillemont, *Histoire Ecclesiastique,* i. 266 ; Calmet's *Dictionaire de la Bible,* verbo Anna ; Sedelmayer, *Theologia Mariana,* No. 151 ; Montague, *Apparatus Biblicus,* Op. 8, Num. 63. The last, a Protestant author, says : " The tradition as to the ancient and primitive names of Joachim and Anna is so well received, that only the rash will oppose so ancient a tradition." Trombelli teaches that Joachim may also have been called Heli, according to the Hebrew custom to have two names. That Anna was also of the royal Davidic line is sustained by Calimus, Binet, and Siandi. The latter says that " Anna was a sister of Jacob, St. Joseph's father." Seldmayr, that " there were three sisters at Bethlehem, daughters of Mathan, a priest, and his wife (Mary) : first, Mary ; next Soba, who married in Bethlehem before Elizabeth ; third, Anne."—Hypolitus in *Nicephorus Hist.,* Lib. i. cap. ii.

6. *Vide* " Nain of Tillemont." The nativity of the B. V. is celebrated by the Latin and Greek churches on the 8th of September. Peter Damon, canonized in the Roman church, reckons the hour of felicitous birth to have been the daybreak. Others add that the sun shone with twofold splendor that morning, and the night preceding the moon appeared without her usual spots, a bright star sparkling on her disc. Considering the predilection of Oriental writers to usher in the births of distinguished personages with the supernatural aurora, it has been a subject of serious reflection whether to give this and kindred traditionary embellishments that may appear both in the notes and text of our little volume ; but we rather opine such occasional glimpses into the remote testimonies or traditional stores of the " Fathers," and theological writers from thence down, will but the more enhance our humble book with the curious, the liberal, and the

candid. " Four cities, viz., Jerusalem, Sephora, Bethlehem, and Naza-
reth, lay claim to her birth-place. Novati and others favor Jerusalem;
Poza, Capero, and other authors of rank, the city of Diocæssarea;
Theophylact, Metaphrastes, and Salmeron, Bethlehem.   We follow
the opinion of those who maintain that Mary was born at Nazareth."
—*Gentilluci.*

7. " I will sing praise unto my God, who has visited me and lifted
me up from the opprobrium of my friends, and given to me the fruit
of justice, multiplied in thy sight.   Hear ye, all ye of my friends!
Hear ye, O sons of Reuben, that Anna rejoices!   Hear ye!   Hear ye!
O ye twelve tribes of Israel, that Anna rejoices!"

8. " Because he was of the house and lineage of David," Luke ii.
4; also Matt. i. 16. The genealogy given by Luke is by some commen-
tators on the Sacred Scriptures considered as the genealogy of Mary,
her genealogy as an only child and a daughter being reckoned unto
her husband, the Jewish custom not admitting of a woman's name
being thus enrolled.

9. According to the learned Francis Suarez, " The priests, as her
father was dead, settled on her state in life . . . . and by light from on
high decided that she should marry one of the same tribe."

10. Gerbet, in his *Lily of Israel*, has the same sentiment illustrated
by the same figures; as we had not, however, seen his book till after
our paragraph was written, nor the imagination elsewhere even
shadowed, we retain the same as equally ours, and for the duplication
of thought and figures, but cherish it the more certainly as a whisper
of the higher inspiration.

11. "A garden now belonging to the village of Jean. A church
now but a heap of ruins was erected upon the site in the middle ages.
Vide *Voyages de Jesus Christ*, p. 4."

12. According to the regulation of David, the priests were divided
into twenty-four courses, each of which in turn served during a week
in the temple at Jerusalem. Zacharias was of the course of Abia.
Vide *Prid. Hist. of the Jews.*

13. The baya-bird lights up her nest at night with fire flies.—
Lalla Rookh.

14. The Virgin, according to Epiphamus, was not tall in stature,
though above the medium height; her countenance, slightly bronzed,
like the countenance of the Sulamite, by the climate of her country,
had that rich glow peculiar to ripe corn . . . . her eyes sparkling with
a black mellow pupil . . . . her lips ruby . . . . the cast of her countenance oval.

BOOK II.

OR

BOOK OF TRIALS.

" YET not the tempest's frown,
Or the delusive smile of stream or flower,
Or painful step on that rude way, had power
    To move her thoughts, whose crown
By angel hands is wove."

CONTENTS.

CHAPTER I.

"AND MARY . . . RETURNED TO HER OWN HOME."

HOME once again! A mother's dear caress!
　　Her kiss—than which, so passionless and pure,
None ever laid on maiden's velvet lip—
And askings for the loved kinswoman left;
A look into the quiet chambered nook,
Couch, curtain, stand, with little silver lamp,
All, as she saw them last; into the vine,
Whose festoons gay clung to the lattice close,
As child to mother-breast. Three months agone,
A nest of yellow straw and moss inwove,
With two smooth shining eggs, swung to the breeze,
That rocked with gentle breath the nested branch.
Browner and birdless hath the pet nest grown;
But there are twitters in the fig tree nigh.
Free wing have they, her lattice birds—not flight.
It is, the very birds seem well to know,

A blessed place in which to nest and sing—
A place no evil can approach to fright.
Now from the cottage porch she comes, of whom
The royal prophet sings, she comes—" her lips
Like scarlet lace, a dropping honeycomb;
Her tastes simple, poetical, and pure;
Who loves to stray the shady vales within,
When vines are in their flower, and the fig tree
Hath put her green leaves forth; a dove her nest
Who builds the crevice of the rocks within,
And veils herself from every eye."
                            She comes—
One hand, arrested, on the wicket lies,
Stayed by the memory that overflows
With softly burning rush.　Sweet garden shades
Thrice sacred evermore and sevenfold blessed.

Through fragrant trees and bloomy bowers
   The gentle south gales blow;
From balmy shrubs and scented flowers
   The spices freely flow.

She seeks, sweet Dove, the grotto blessed,
Where Gabriel's shining foot hath pressed;
Mute sit the song birds on the spray,
While lovely Mary kneels to pray.

CHAPTER II.

COTTAGE-BUILDING.

"JOSEPH THE CARPENTER."

SCENE—*Early morning.*

THROUGH the rich transparent air,
  Nature's hymning voice of prayer
Breaks and quavers everywhere.

Round the flower bud's nectared cell,
  From the busy bees a-thrumming,
  From the honey birds a-humming,
  From the noisy beetles drumming,
Thick the active murmurs swell.

Tuning in with silvery singing
Falls a hammer, clearly ringing,
Ringing on the fir and cedar,
Stately trees from Hermon's brow;
Beating with the cunning hammer,
Drowning half the morning clamor,
  Breaking forth in psalm-word choice,
Bursting forth in chantings grand,
  Flows a clear and manly voice;

Till the liquid notes they rush
In a full and golden gush.
" Praise the Lord of earth and Heaven !
I will love thee, O my strength !
Loving kindness ! loving kindness,
Falls on David, his anointed,
And his seed forevermore !
Praise the Lord of earth and Heaven !
Praise the Lord of earth and Heaven ! "

In the majesty of palms,
And extravagance of flowers,
In the brilliance of the morn,
Song, with beauty everywhere ;
Man and bird and bee,
Nature's minstrelsy,
Life and love and singing,
Song and worship everywhere.

Veteran workman ! rest thee now ;
Stop to wipe the beaded brow ;
Pause while sultry tropics shower
Down the floods of sun-tide hour ;
Pause and seek the shaded pool,
Where the fountains sparkle cool ;

Here the burning thirst to slake,
Here the frugal meal to take,
White bread from thy basket store,
Juicy fruits ripe to the core,
A little bag of crackled corn,
And honeycomb, fresh took at morn.
Feast and rest! and muse and smile!
I will paint thy thought the while.

Joseph.

I have almost framed the bower,
Where I will transplant my flower;
Where my Love-Rose bright shall bloom,
Where my Lily shed her rare perfume.
I will build its chambers fair,
I will carve each winding stair,
And the trellised palisade
With the vine and aloe shade;
Here anemones shall blow,
Here the rose of Jericho,
Till surrounds it everywhere
Tree and shrub and garden fair;
Then before the lilies blow
Next around this fountain's flow,
Glad, my Mary I will call
Sweet to queen it over all;

Maid as marvellous as fair!
She shall be my household saint.

Who is he that frames the cottage,
Dreams beside the pool of lilies,
In the shadow of the palms,
And who names the name of Mary?
Is he worthy? Is he worthy?
He who weds the Rose of Jesse
Pure should be in flesh and spirit;
He should be more saint than human,
More an angel than a man.

  Look up, Judah's lordly line!
  Line of patriarch and king;
  At the foot of Jacob's ladder,
  See a name that's written "just."
  What a word magnificent!
  Written with Jehovah just!
  Just with God, he is worthy:
  God's elect are always worthy.

CHAPTER III.

FOREBODINGS.

"ONE IS MY DOVE, MY PERFECT ONE IS BUT ONE; SHE IS THE ONLY ONE OF HER MOTHER, THE CHOSEN OF HER THAT BORE HER."—CANTICLES.

(Scene in Anna's cottage.)

TURNING the barley cake, just large enough
For two to sup from with a full content,
The pious Anna lifts her heart in prayer.

ANNA.

I thank thee, Father, thou art still
The widow's God, the husband unto me;
Bless'd is my basket and my store—enough!
My fatherless claims heavenly care, my child!
My darling child! Heaven keep her well! Heaven
    shield!
There have of late forebodings sad and strange
Been knocking at my watchful heart. Nay, nay,
It cannot be! the bud I've in my bosom lain
And nurtured into bloom! the fairest rose
Of Judah's royal tree—it cannot nurse
The worm of canker at its fragrant heart!

Yet, yet, I've heard; have from tradition heard
Of those, who've walked the golden streets and sat
The shadow of the sapphire walls beneath,
Who've listened to the tempter's voice without.
When angels bright from the pure heavens down-drop
Defiled, with timid feet let woman walk.
Heaven keep my loveliest, my child! nor let
The shadow of a sin her pure brow cloud.

The browned cake smokes upon the waiting board;
The same sweet, sacred Mary at the door,
Who sat the fair pomegranate tree beneath,
And Gabriel blessed, as woman blessedest,
Comes, with all the woman and the angel,
In look, in step, the cottage-floor across,
And lays from the grape-basket in her hand
A cluster on the nicely crusted cake.
A mystery like the drapery of her robe—a veil
Of heaven floats round her softly luminous,
And dims the curious search of human eyes.
Peace with her presence comes.   The present God
Is felt.   And pious Anna breaks their bread
With thanks.

CHAPTER IV.

AMONG THORNS.

PART I.

" AND HE WAS MINDED TO PUT HER AWAY PRIVILY."—MATT. i. 17.
" AS THE LILY AMONG THORNS."—CANTICLES.

THE harvest time had come.
There was a sound of sickles in the field ;
The earth gave back her bearded gifts with toil ;
And hardiest reaper in the sweltering plain,
Cheered by the bright-eyed gleaner in his wake,
Bent blither to the task, forgetting not
To let some goodly ear his sheaf escape.
And all went merry for the harvest feast :
Such was the husbandry without ; within,
Abstractedly her dreamy fingers lost
Among a half-wrought sandal's silken threads,
Thought drifting back unto the day she traced
That pattern of fine lily-work—Virgin
Of Jesse, upon the rustic bench of stone,
The palm-tree awning of the quiet porch
Above her sacred head—she sits and thinks
How careful she had pointed every leaf,

Traced every stem (it was her bridal shoe),
And rounded out each little bell that day—
The task she scarcely heeds to finish now,
So rapt the soul content with God—she sits
And thinks of that one day, o'erwhelming bright,
And days all deepening since in blessedness,
The day to come—betrothed by God and led
By His sweet Spirit will, betrothed to man,
All revelations left to God, His hour—
She sits, O, radiant maid! with beauteous head
Low-bent as saint at prayer, or cherub bright
In shadow of the Throne.　I see her thus,
Bright-thoughted eyes in musings rich downcast,
Till the rapture-bloomed cheek the brown lash swept,
And half-parted mouth curved with the deep thought s
Slowly and eloquently welling up
Unto those lips grace-touched with constant glow
Of heaven, breathing, even in silence, but
Odors of holiness to shed.

　　　　　　　　　"Oh, God!
How beautiful!" sighs one.　Joseph, the Just,
Has drawn anear, unseen, his eyes unloosed;
Like some tall palm by deadly simoom struck
He stands—"Just God! and can it be?　The woman
Whom I've loved and worshipped as a saint!"

JOSEPH.

Ah, Mary, I would sooner looked to have seen
The mountain tree change its living green!
The plant perennial lose its wonted bloom,
Fade with the year and seek a winter tomb!
Or lily from its bell of snowy white
Unroll an odious sable flower to sight!
Oh, what is woman's faith, her truth, her love?
Brief as the rainbow's painted arch above,
That glows a moment gloriously bright,
Then melts in beauty on the ravish'd sight!
False as the glitter of the jeweled wave
That sparkles o'er the wrecked one's yawning grave!
Her truth, like silver net-work on the flowers
That passes with the Orient's purpled hours!
Her love, sure as the poisoned nectar-cup,
Death to the lips that drain its sweetness up!

[Never a word the stainless Virgin speaks—
Never a word—with face too white for words.]

JOSEPH.

Had all cried out, Thy bride is false to thee!
With anchored trust in thy pure constancy,
I would the bitter taunt have coldly hurled
With unmoved scorn back to an envious world.

3

But, ah, mine eyes they see ! this stricken heart
Receives the stab and writhes beneath the smart !

[Never a word the stainless Virgin speaks—
Never a word—with face too white for words.]

JOSEPH.

There is within our just Mosaic laws
One that now gapes for thee its iron jaws.
Oh, had I reverenced ne'er as almost lips divine,
The lips that kissed with me betrothal wine,
I back might hurl the envenomed shaft,
And thou might'st lip the false one's fatal draught !

[Large tears are in those blessed eyes ! Large tears
Drop on those lovely cheeks.   Tears, but not words.]

JOSEPH.

Nay, thou art safe ; this tongue could ne'er proclaim
So public to a mocking world such shame.
I cannot take thee to my arms my bride,
But privately, I will cast thee aside.

In growing grief, one other gaze he took ;
In pious sorrow then her side forsook.

PART II.

O, Mary, sweet Mary, on the bench of stone,
Does she love, and that man in the noon of his years,[1]
Who hath smote her with words so hot and sharp,
And turned in such haste from her door?

She loves as the angels love,
And that man in the strength of his years:
The love that over a chasm leaps,
Upward or down, is strong:
It tallies in sooth not years, but counts
Only the jewel dimmed is old:
It reckons only the age of heart:
And she loves, as the angels love,
With a love more deep than the love of the flesh,
That man of the patriarchs most pure,
That man who has turned in grief from her door.

PART III.

"GOD IS IN THE MIDST OF HER."

When the winds with the cedars talk,
When the strong old oaks of the Bashan hills
Are hugged in the arms of the storm,
As the dove to the cleft of the rock,

To her garden enclosed,
This Dove of the Ark,
Bearing the olive-branch, peace,
Escapes from the storm
To her altar of rock.

Above where she kneels,
Straight over her head,
There's a spot in the sky
Where the blue lights up;
Where God looks through.
Hush!   The Father looks through
On his daughter below,
And a halo falls over her head.

And the illuminating God is there;
The presence of the bright celestial spouse
Shines even o'er the ground on which she kneels:
O, holy place!   The very angels draw
In tender reverence back:
"The holy place of the tabernacle of the most Highest,
God is in the midst of her, therefore shall she not be
Removed; God shall help her, and that right early."

CHAPTER V.

CONSECRATION.—NIGHT.

"THOU ART ALL FAIR, MY LOVE, THERE IS NO SPOT IN THEE."—CANTI-
CLES iii. 8.

SCENE—*Midnight in Anna's Cottage.*

DIM was the mother's eye with tears suppress'd;
By her warm hearth she sat, nor felt the glow
The ruddy embers flickering cast on stone,
And wall, and her.   Her child!   Fain would
She wake and find it but a nightmare grief;
Some demon must have stole the blossom fair,
The sweet young flower she'd nourished at her breast.
Ah, how convictions sore had wrestled sharp
Ere they prevailed, while silence, like a seal
Of heaven, had locked her lips against rebuke,
Or such sad questioning.   How could she ask?
And now she sits pride crushed, a mother's pride,
So loving it is blameless quite.   She sits,
Love for her child, the last flower of her life,
Bleeds at her heart.   With a less sickening grief
She could have laid that sweetest head, Oh, God!
Upon its youthful bier, unspotted down.

Yet, not to love, to shield, now her betrothed
Had turned with chidings her heart froze to hear—
Ah, sterner man hath not a mother's heart.

O, spring of love, by living waters fed !
    With all the blessed fulness of its worth ;
    It trembles when it gushes into birth ;
    Yet, 'neath the cloud it gathers power,
    Most mighty in misfortune's hour ;
O, spring of love, by living waters fed !

Her precious child *was* pure, was beautiful—
Some subtle fiend must strange possession hold ;
Yet she must love—must love for what *has been.*
O, conflict strange ! why speaks His angel not ?
Shall such indignity of thought cast cloud
O'er the sweet Ark of Covenant that bears
The pure Incarnate Word within ?
                         The rose,
Its roots in earth, remains a rose intact ;
The cloud above no shadow leaves on snow ;
The pure, with touch, suspicion cannot spot.
The ways of God we fathom not ;
Yet this—this much we learn, and soon, His Cross,
The Christ, all who come near, must somewhere touch.

But who is she that cometh from her chamber forth?

" Her coming forth aerial as the odor of perfumes; her beauty vieing with the rising of the moon." Solomon traces her with his pencil: " She is selected for a mystical marriage in preference to the queens and virgins of every other nation; a crown is promised her by him who loveth her soul, and the happy bond by which she is united to her royal spouse is stronger than death."

MARY.

My mother, dear,
The night air groweth chill, the embers die
Upon the hearth; the midnight cricket sings;
My mother, dear, the harvest moon rides high.

ANNA.

The moon? I've often watched of late—*the moon!*

MARY.

Methinks the moon was made our couch to watch,
And thus in trust we sleep.

ANNA.

But I watch hers.
When all things change, why not the moon and I?

MARY.

For wherefore best, that sleep is dew to life,
And sheds the glows of heaven in dreams,

And nightly comes to make us slow acquaint,
Softly and slow before it comes with death.
'Tis writ, " He giveth his beloved sleep."
Sweet text.

ANNA.

Sleep then, poor child, sleep while thou canst.

MARY.

From pillowed rest, from couch that held me charmed
Ere Philomel, drugged with the drowsy sweetness
Of her song, forgot her notes and fell a-doze,
I rose as something whispered through my heart,
' Thy mother wakes.'

ANNA.

And did it tell she wakes
To weep ?—and has her last delight outlived ?

MARY.

Outlived ! for us the fair millennial dawns !
Such sorrowing doubt, why wears thy tearful eye ?
My mother questions whom?   God, or her child ?
Has no sure angel whisper spoken her
Of mystery we may not seek to ken ?

On God, cannot the pious Anna lean,
And leave with Him her child?   With Him,
Hid in the safe pavilion of his love,
The Everlasting arms are round about.

ANNA.

With God?   God!   God!
     [And questioning, her eye
Ran o'er the form that 'twixt her and the lamp
In wane enhaloed by a growing light
In wondrous beauty half-draped stood.]

The tender tremblings of a virgin heart,
The sweet, resplendent maid one moment shook,
But straight the peace that fell was like a cloud
Of love.   The spreading halo filled the room;
Our scene, unto a Raphael picture like,
" Commences on the earth but finishes
The clouds within."   As martyr Stephen saw
The heavens unroll and open on his view,
So pious Anna upward looked, and saw
The mother of Messias at her feet :
Heard words too holy to be wrote outpoured,
Until her eye uplifted as a star,
And prophet-like the loving, reverent hand
Lay on the consecrated head that leaned
For parent-blessing on her happy knees.

  3*

CHAPTER VI.

REVELATION.

"BUT WHILE HE THOUGHT OF THOSE THINGS."—MATTHEW.
"HE THAT IS THE KEEPER OF HIS LORD SHALL BE GLORIFIED."—ISAIAH.

JOSEPH—a name that in translation reads
  "Protection," or "a tree that's beautiful,"
The Providence that gives to trees exposed
Their depth of root, and tries their majesty
Of strength, when from their dens where leopards
    house
The winds unloose, and fills their boughs with stern
And solemn calm as creeps the muttering storm
Into its mountain cavern jaded back,
That Providence this human tree hath shook,
In which all patriarchal virtues shone;
And now the moon of harvest looketh in
Where patient Joseph in his silent grief
Fills earth and heaven with admiration vast;
While doubting as a man that God may speak,
And henceforth put all cavil to the shame,
Bowed low in meek submission as a saint,
He wavers not.   His mind is fixed;
Still in its very fixedness a pain,

A cold, deep pain, that urns each sacred hope.
The admiration that with reverence blends,
And her by her rare sanctity become
The charm of his affections pure, he yields
To God ; that love of which none lovelier line
Were wrote, "Love is its own true loveliness,"
That love can yield its idol but to God,
And smile again on earth.   Just man, his heart
Is sacrificed ; and yet the drowsy lids—
God sendeth sleep—droop o'er the drowsy eyes.
Mysterious sleep ! stand by, and watch God's work ;
See how His sleep comes to you every night :
Soft, steeping stupor stealing sluggish, slow
Along the jaded nerves, numb fingers
On the plastic form sinking by pressure
Of hand unseen, down the void depths of sleep.
Half imperceptible, and weak, and faint,
Struggling a weary moment with its fate,
The timid captive shrinks a-startled back ;
But every limb is sleepy now, the brain
Inebriating, staggers at its watch,
The broad chest heaves, the labored breath pants up,
And mind, lost to itself, rests unaware.
Then from its blank outleaps the restive brain,
Tableauing wonderous images that glide,
Like panoramic views in by the soul

That sees as clear as through its human eyes.
O, mystery! that images both life
And death, with subtle argument for both.
But still there lies a dead weight at his heart,
Darkening the foreground of his dream, till, lo!
A fleecy brightness like unto a cloud
Of snowy whiteness, fills the expanding room.
The pillows lift; the narrow walls and thatch
Of palm in silent grandeur rise and spread,
And, lost in light, stand in the distance back,
Half indistinct, a flowing robe in air infolds;
From midst outbeams a brow serenely fair,
And touch, unseen the eyes of vision thrill;
And Joseph sees an angel in his dream,
The angel of the Lord, and hears him say,
' Fear not, O David's son, *'tis of the Lord.*'

From darkness, doubt, and pain, O, bright transfer,
Too sweet! too rapt! too luminous for words!
The vision melts—but, lo! the joy is left!
The chosen spouse of that prophetic bride!
The foster-father of the Christ unborn!
The vision it has passed, but, lo! the joy is left.

    And through all the watches nightly
    Came the angel whispers softly,

' Take her ! take her ! she is holy,
Take, but touch not, take not wholly ;
Let no breath of passion faintly,
Soil the lips so rapt and saintly ;
Wife in name, but pure evangel,
She can love but as thy angel ;
She is woman sealed, but tender,
Let no wanton wish offend her ;
High and pure her trust as Heaven,
Let such care in turn be given.
Take her ! take her ! she is holy ;
Take, but touch not, take not wholly.'
Thus through all the waches nightly,
Came the angel whispers softly.

————+————

CHAPTER VII.

CHANGES.

"THE LORD GIVETH, THE LORD TAKETH."

IT was a Syrian morn, and Syrian morns are fair :
The pearl-cloud blushed a rose, and straight the rose
Crimsoned upon the golden-breasted sky,
Where constant for a thousand years or more

To the rich bosom that he glorified,
The sun upon the verge-cloud dipped and pressed,
Pillowed one moment lavishingly there,
Then rising brighter, prouder up, walked to his work;
The giant firs on Carmel's shaggy brow
First lit, the Cades palms their floodings took
Like crowns, and sweet the rose of Jericho
Opened her glowing bosom to the morn.
For grace, exalted like the Cades palm,
For love, than rose of Jericho more sweet,
The Virgin mother of the Christ unborn,
Looks from her casement on the growing morn,
Marks the ascending sun—of prophecy
The child, yet all the creature lost in God—
'O Sun of Righteousness (she silent prays),
Earth waits Thy rise! Thy rise with healing wings!
When will her shadows flee, her morning come?
Lord, let the moments haste!' and, swayed with rush
Of holy tenderness, she stood—I cannot say
How long. The pulses of the heart that beat
Above the Christ, are not for us to count;
But, sweetly visioned, this I reverent tell:
Her cheek was fairer than the morn, her lip,
The breath that on it lay was love, her eye—
But sudden shadow o'er its brightness fell,

As the matin breeze did blow
To her ear a whisper low:
Mary, blessed, thou shouldst know

Soon will pale the Orient's beam,
Fading fast the rosiest gleam,
Mornings are not what they seem!

E'en the dew-pearls of the thorn
Breathe away with wasting morn;
All things perish earthly born.

In on her rapt thoughts like a knell of earth,
A sudden knell, it broke, and low she knelt,
As the white lily of the valley bows
Its head when storms are in the summer air.

Then rose in all her wondrous meekness up,
And spirit-calmed, to take life's unknown cup.
                    (*Mary at the door of Anna's chamber.*)
Again that sighing angel whisper, soft!
                    (*Mary within the chamber of Anna.*)
' And she is dead ! '

                    O God ! for sorrow was
She stayed, prepared, yet not for *this !*

Sad is the first death-chill that sudden falls
On fresh young hearts; severing of tenderest ties
Hath pain, though angel-wings the smote brow fan,
And heavenly lips touch soothingly the wound;
Still mutely looks God's orphan up; her heart
Is wrung; her jealous God her last earth-prop
Removes; yet all her bleeding thoughts but fly
To Him.   Its own beloved, Heaven answers quick.
There is a hurried footfall in the porch,
And on the floor.   He who but yesternoon
Had cast her off, greets more than tenderly;
One drop of love is in the bitter draught;
She hearkens unto one the Lord hath sent.

Joseph.

Know thou, our Lord has taken but His own
To Abram's glorious bosom but before—
" She comes to us no more "—we upward tend
Toward Heaven and her; be comforted and bless
His holy name who kindly gives, and takes
As kind.   O death-touched lips, soft chilled in smile!
Sweet breathing still—that smile—as Moses died
When he the distant Canaan shore o'erlooked,
Our sainted mother bright in dying caught
Of our Messiah's coming kingdom view.

(Turning toward Mary.)

O, sacredest of women! God grant me
To be sire, husband, mother unto thee!

And opening wide his generous, pitying arms,
She took their shelter like a child, and long
Upon his shielding breast wept free such loss.
And when the green sods wrapped the precious dead,
He led her to his home.[2]

NOTES TO BOOK II.

1. IT is probable that when St. Joseph married the Blessed Virgin, he was neither young nor old, but of mature age.—Capizucas, *Controv. Theologiæ Selectæ*. In ancient paintings, Joseph is generally represented as far advanced in years—an aged, patriarchal man. The authorities, however, that we have consulted, favor mostly the opinion that he was rather in the meridian of life, which is harmonious with our contemplation of the man appointed for the protection of the mother and child, not only in Nazareth and Bethlehem, but in their flight unto and sojourn in Egypt; and while the Scripture record bears no certain proof, it lacks not ground for such inference: hence, we follow fair Scriptural ground for argument, and a fair, sustained current of tradition.

2. Espousals among the Hebrews were what marriage is among us. The husband had power over his spouse as a wife. To consummate the marriage required only some formalities, as leading the betrothed to her husband's house. The Jews called spouses those whom we call married, but without some solemnities which are often postponed as not essential to the union.—Calmet, *Dictionary of the Bible, verbo Mary*. "The Bollandists record, that the city of Perugia has the nuptial ring of Mary kept in a gold shrine with eleven keys, which has its own appropriate feast."

BOOK III.

OR

THE HOLY INFANCY.

" Not o'er the kingly halls,
Where regal mothers from their couch of down
Gaze on the heir of some imperial crown,
     The golden glory falls,

.   .   .   .   .   .

     But in a narrow shed
Yet fragrant with the breath of lowing kine,
Rested its glorious beams   .   .
     Around an infant's head—
     A little new-born child;

.   .   .   .

And calmly on the Virgin-Mother's knee
     The mighty Saviour smiled."

CONTENTS.

CHAPTER I.

BIRTH-NIGHT.

> " There is no tie on earth
>   To which affection may give birth
>   Dearer than that of mother :
>
>   .   .   .   .   .
>
>   And if it thus give birth
>   To the best feelings of this earth,
>   It surely should enchain our love
>   To Thee,   .   .   .
>   Thou lily of fair purity,
>   Thou the dear Saviour's mother."

PART I.

LONG caravans crowd Bethlehem's narrow gates,
    (To tax the world a Cæsar has decreed,)
They who the golden harvests gather in,
Who the red vintage tread, or watch their flocks
Upon the neighboring hills, her peasant sons.
Yet nigh thy gates, O humble Bethlehem,
Are guests whose sojourn shall unto thee bring

A glory and renown that shall not fade
And pass away like glories of the earth.
Rejoice! rejoice, O happy Bethlehem![1]
"*He comes!*" the cradle of the Christ prepare!

Across the plain, a man of reverent brow
And wealth of generous looks, guides on a mule
On which a woman sits, her head in veil
Bowed weariedly adown unto the bridle-rein,
Whom tenderly the anxious husband speaks:
' We're almost there.   Beloved, cheer thee up;
In sight, the walls of Bethlehem heave up.'

Come to the town—no place is found. "Full! full!"
The bustling keeper of the inn proclaims.
Nor couch, nor shelter, save an empty crib,
Within a manger where two heifers stall ;
And meekest Mary gladly sinks, a bed
Of harvest straw, upon.   That night the Christ,
The Saviour of the world, was in a manger born ;
And it was in the heavenly records wrote,
Gold-lettered on the book of God, Birth-Night.
The Sole Begotten One in Bethlehem born.

PART II.

At midnight hour, olden tradition saith,
An angel-chant on Joseph's slumber brake,
When rising from his couch the door anear,
Flooded with brightness softly glorious,
He wondering saw the caverned [2] manger glow,
And Mary seated on the yellow straw,
With countenance all radiant with joy,
Swathing her new-born babe—in worship mute
The two white heifers kneeling at her feet;
While singing angels, hovering o'er her head,
Fanned with their golden wings the holy twain:
——————————————————————and rapt
With glory of the vision grew entranced.

MEDITATION.

This scene, I've written it out once. I've written it out twice. Part I. A painting of St. Luke, recorded on his gospel page. Part II. A picture that in mystic book I found, and my heart to it grew and could not give it back—and now much moved to write it thrice. I pause, and wherefore seek? Perchance for cause it is so fair, —at each stand-point so fair unrolls—so freshly fair first glimpse of God Incarnate seen—nor cross, nor shadow yet, only the " Child." " The child is given," and " God with us." Or yet, perchance the consciousness awakes, and instant grows desire that travails to outbring in perfectness the vision of the soul, and clings enamored to the subtle sense, " the half not told." Not told; ay, true, indeed, where one wants words of heaven, and has but earth's, there picture comes out slow, and holds at best the difference up between

4

the glory of a thought unspoke and wrote. But so it comes; God
giveth thoughts and we choose words. He holds the picture up before the soul and leaves us there. And yet there is a joy with this
poor weakness for to wrestle well—and I am moved to write this scene
again—to write it thrice, and give it to you each; but let me, while
I prose, here mark, nor do I dare indulge a hope so high, or rather
put it sweet, for God knows how I'm lowly grateful for my theme;
and while it floods, yet how it keeps me low; and I might never
dream a hope so sweet, as that my pencil poor, should it out-trace
this scene a thousand times, could ever give of one a rounded
whole. I rather here opine, I still should but confess "the half not
told." And yet, I pray, allow me now to linger at this Bethlehem
one hour more, and I will sum excuses all in this—I love to write,
and only write for love, and therefore must.

Musing on this Bethlehem of old,
Watching at its manger-door,
O, this glorious first Christmas !
O, this mysterious sweet Christmas !
Hidden half, and half revealed,
How its mysteries swell my reverence,
How its visions charm my seeing,
Watching at its manger-door !

Picture first as it rises
Without stain of care or labor,
Ere the angels light their lanterns,
Or the stars walk out in splendor,
To o'erlook the Bethlehem manger,

Gathering rest from day-gone travel,
Sleeping as the honest weary,
Kindly, patriarchal Joseph,
Guards the threshold still in sleep.

Ere the stars walk out in splendor
To o'erlook the Bethlehem manger,
Gathering all her freshness back,
Gathering strength for the great joy
That the midnight holds so near,
Sleeps the royal Rose of Jesse,
Sleeps the sweetest rose of woman;
Cheek of tender womanhood,
Fair as rind of the young cinnamon,
Sleeping, but on earth and straw:
Oh, has earth no better keeping
For its sole unspotted maiden?
Sweet on straw as down of eider
Sleeps the lily-maid of Israel,
Sleeps the loveliest of women.

Oh, has earth no better birth-place
For her coming Lord and Saviour?

Cattle on a thousand hills,
Earth's the Lord's and all its fulness,

Down through kingly David's kingly psalms,
Still to-day is grandly singing:
" Earth's the Lord's and all its fulness ! "
Earth has nought to do in choosing.

And runneth thus the argument of God I read: As things, both
are alike with God; as used, the manger it hath kept its primal white,
than purest palace whiter far. Thus Heaven delights to golden
earth's humility, and lift the meek ; unto its veriest nothingness to
come and say, ' I who made crowns, made poverty, and 'tis as good
with me as gold, and so much holier far, I choose it out from all
the purples of the world as dower for my sole Son.'

Hark !   I hear the angels sing !
Shall I tell you what they sing,
Seated round her couch of straw ?
What the vesper angels sing
In this Bethlehem of yore ?

(*Angels sing.*)

Sleep, belovedest of women !
From the wayside flush and fever,
Rest in this poor cave of earth,
He will make it heaven for thee ;
          God is wondrous !
          God is good !
Sleep, belovedest of women,
He will make it heaven for thee.

While the vesper angels sing,
         Softly sing,
And the cave is brightened softly,
         Softly brightened,
To this angel-circled couch,
Draw anear, my soul, with reverence,
With a loving, tender reverence;
Bless thy God—Bless His Christ;
Name His name, and draw anear.

'Tis the same sweet vision,
Sweeter—dearer—brightened!   But,
'Tis the same sweet vision.
  A woman's face pillows on straw,
         Rarest and sweetest
  That as yet earth ever saw.

    Study that countenance,
    Drink in its beauty,
    A brow like an angel,
    Lips like the pomegranate,
    Earth's sweetest evangel;
    Yet, that's not its beauty,
    'Tis the glow in the face
    Of this mystical moon,
    'Tis the light of her Sun,

Unrisen to earth,
Enhaloes her head—
Sweet hidden with her,
Illumines her face,
Encircles her lips,
And shines through the cheek
Transparent as truth,
As she dreams of her babe,
And yearneth to clasp ;
'Tis the glow in her face
As she yearns for her babe.

But I dizzy with the brightness,
And the hours I fail to count
As I stand back in the shadows
Waiting at the manger-door
Of this Bethlehem of yore,
But, I hear the angels singing,
Hear them even in my blindness,
In the sweetest angel-murmur
Singing softly—singing raptly,
Circled round that couch of straw,
' Sleep, belovedest of women.'

Trembling through a break of song,
Reverentful, angel-whisper,

Than the rising of a thought,
In those angel-breasts or mine,
Louder, scarcely—angel-whisper,
' He will be born ! be born to-night !
A virgin-maid a mother be ! '

Softer drops the melody—
' God is wonderful !
God is good ! '
Softer drops the melody
From the angel-lip entranced—
Drops till lost in sweetness,
Drops till lost in awe,
Lost in awe, lost in sweetness,
" *God is love !* "

Silent ; for the glory near,
From their wings shedding sanctities,
As the odor from the rose
Wafted only,
Sleep belovedest of women !

" MY BELOVED TO ME AND I TO HIM."

The stars tell twelve—"Twelve of the night !" the angel cries
who counts the hours. " *He comes !*"—" *The Word made flesh* "—
the " Light "—" *And this is the true light that lighteth every man
that cometh into the world.*" And all the angels sing.

A vision glows that beggars words—
   Queen of the blessed,
   Mother of purity,
   Mother of a Son that is Infinite,
Smile on my dimness and turn it to light!

   The raptest human face,
   The raptest human face I see,
The daughter of the patriarchs in sweetest adoration
   Bending o'er her bright Messiah-Babe!
   Feasting on His beauty,
   Beauty the divinest!
   Beauty celestial!
   Seeing her features,
   Her own lovely features,
   In the face of The Babe;
   Her own lovely features
   In the face of her Babe
   Lit with a radiance,
   The radiance of Deity!
   The soft-burning radiance of Deity.

   Look on this picture;
   See her feast on His beauty;
   Learn of her how to love!
   Learn of her how to worship!
How to worship, to love, and adore!

Mother of the Incarnation!   All sweet hails!
Ave Maria!   Ave Maria!

Mother of the Incarnation! first of the human race to see God in the flesh! God to see! God to touch! God to kiss! first! *first!*

O, woman, first to taste the apple false!

O, woman, first to kiss the Son,

And give to man more than he lost!

The brighest seraph in the band that rings the Throne

Would lay his crown down for that joy!

Men nor angels, they can never

Honor thee as God to night.

And yet thou sittest there as meek with thy Messiah-Babe upon thy knees as the lily on which God looks in heaven. That drinks the glory of His look, stands an irradiated flower; but stands in its chaste brightness richly still, and never thinks to lift its head, and gives unconscious back the sweetness from its tender, white, illumined leaves, and God enjoys. Thus Mary-Mother, her pure virgin face aglow, mutely o'erbends and feasts. O, mothers, ye who feed your first-born at your breasts, with eyes that meanwhile feed upon your babes, until from their transparent depths the tender sheddings breathe "no love like this," your babe is no more yours; and she who nearer cometh in the flesh, in spirit-sympathy, as nearer, nearly draws unto the Christ, and there abides, than sweetest saint may ever hope to draw. Nor saint, nor angel ever loved like her. Mutely o'erbent, O, there is love enough to move a world in those two eyes that gaze down on that Babe. Such love, and such humility! O, adorative love! O, marvellous humility! "He has exalted the humble!" And now her hand, her soft hand, touches lovingly, lovingly—reverently touches.

4*

MARY.

A mortal, and a God!

Son of the Highest!

God! God!

Son of the Highest!

Son of the Highest, and *mine!*

I worship thee, God!

Babe from the heavens!

Babe begotten of Heaven,

Which wilt thou, my Dove,

My beautiful Dove!

My sweet, sacred Dove!

Worship or care?

A slave to adore Thee,

Or a mother to fold Thee?

My heart yearns for thee, Babe;

I offer Thee both,

My breast and my prayer.

The sweet Messiah-Babe that lieth still upon her lap unswathed, warm with the " clinging glow of Heaven ; " she wraps Him in her unbound hair. It goldens with the touch. Her robe of russet brown grows beautified. Each splintered straw of that poor couch takes edge of gold. Crib, cave, ragged rock-walls, seam, fissure, stand out englorified. Man, woman, beasts, all that the Eden represented here, and God with them. The glow of heaven o'er all.

MARY.

My heart yearns for thee, Babe!

I offer Thee both,

My breast and my prayer!

" My Beloved unto me and I unto him! "

And with the glow off-shedding from her hair that tender wraps the bright Immanuel-Babe, she gathers Him unto her breast. She folds Him to her heart, and feels the heart of God beat back to hers, and in her transports kisses Him a thousand times. "Kiss me with the kisses of thy mouth, for thy love is sweeter than wine!" O, raptured mother of the Christ new-born! thou kissest Him. I cannot write a sweeter thing, and herewith dot Amen.

CHAPTER II.

WATCH OF THE SHEPHERDS.

" KEEPING WATCH OVER THEIR FLOCKS BY NIGHT."—LUKE ii. 8–15.

LOW bleatings from the folds come softly borne
    At intervals with hollow tinkle-sound
From restive leader's bell. The watch-fires gleam,
The fleecy smoke in blue and dusky wreath
Floats curling slow in all fantastic shapes
Up through the thin cold air, and shepherds hold
The timely watch " all seated on the ground."

" Timely "—at night-hour comes the jackall's cry,
Or tiger prowls for first unguarded lamb,
Or cowardly hyena hath been seen
At twilight skulking in the outskirt hedge.
Circling the seer-eyed patriarch of the band,
The simple keepers of the fold lend ear,
Their seer, uplifted to the star-bright heavens
His face, wrinkled and weird, yet eloquent
With truths from nature and from God, long read,
And reading still, as drifts his searching sight,
Eye-flooded with the breaking prophecy,
Up to the growing glory-pregnant skies.

SEER.

Look, shepherds, forth upon the night-garbed earth,
And up where clay-clogged footsteps never track,
Count yonder stars, name Deity's vast works,
And sum the grandeurs of the Infinite.
See ye one vacant place—room for one star?
Lies on thy dumb-hushed mouth, O shepherd men,
The spell and awe-charm of the shade begot
And brought forth 'neath the altars of the stars?
Nay, more, the mystery in heaven unspoke?
See ye one vacant place, room for one star?
Great is the Lord who giveth stars and place!
O night! black night! illumined night!

The creamy day-dawn fair, high-noon a-blaze,
Or sunset crimson-bloomed, when God out-reaches
His great hand and paints the evening skies,
Heaves never such flood-tides of the sublime
Up o'er the thought-raised peaks of looming mind !
And this night moveth more than erst :
I cannot word the why :—we wait for God.

Not a 'larum from the wold,
Not a bleating from the fold,
Not a crackle from the flame,
Not a breath of question came,
Not an air-breeze moved to stir
Topmost branch upon the fir,
Soul-astonished all and still,
Waiting for the Higher Will,
Till before the wondering sight
Broke the vision of the night.
Golden-robed in flooding light,
Stood a towering angel bright,
Shinings from whose robe and crown
Lit the dewy herbage round,
Till within its dazzling rays
Paled the lighted fagot's blaze,
And o'er shepherd, fold, and plain
Played a lambent glory-flame ;

Grouped in fear upon the sod,
Manhood's pulse forgot its throb,
Bodings to each stout heart came,
Quakings shook each stalworth frame
Till the glorious "*peace!*" was said:
' Shepherds, wherefore bow afraid ?
Unto Israel 's born a king!
Tidings joyful, lo! I bring!
Let all nations of the earth
Triumph in His righteous birth,
Hail their Saviour, Christ the Lord,
Promised in the Heavenly word;
Prince Immanuel's birth below,
Go and welcome, shepherds, go!'

As such heavenly message broke,
As such angel-word was spoke,
In the greatness of surprise
Lifting up their startled eyes,
Suddenly through parted cloud
Burst a raptured angel-crowd,
Tidings of the Heavenly birth
Singing midst the heavens and earth;
Till the starry regions rang,
This the song the angels sang,

Thus the seraph-anthem ran :
" *Heaven's good-will from God to man.*"
And while each immortal wing
Nearer did its radiance fling,
Sweeter surged through rifted sky
Rolled the angel-music nigh,
' Glory ! glory ! glory ! '
(Chorus of the angel-story),
" *Glory to the Highest.   Glory !* "
' Glory ! glory ! glory ! '

(Singing thrice.)

' Heaven's good-will from God to man,
Peace to thee, O troubled earth,
Joy in thy Redeemer's birth,
Glory ! glory ! glory !
" *Glory to the Highest !* "   Glory !
Glory ! glory ! glory ! '

CHAPTER III.

SEEKING THE MANGER.

PART I.

"AS THE ANGELS WERE GONE AWAY FROM THEM INTO HEAVEN."—LUKE ii.

> Soaring aloft their chant swells high and clear,
> Till slow its echo dies within each hill,
> Till the last murmur's lost upon the ear,
> And all around the sheepfold has grown still.
> > MANZONI'S *Ode on the Nativity.*

SHEPHERD SEER.

ANGEL-counsel let us take,
　　Let us heed the angel-sign,
Seek the heir of David's line.

And they come.　It is scarce the middle watch betwixt the midnight and the morn; and yet there is a blessed brightness in the night.　The birds see it, and twitter in "the moist branches of the fig trees" as they pass.　They come.　And, what bear ye, O shepherd men?　Unto the Christ-feet, what?　Spice from the forest?　Myrrh from the mountain?　Gold from the mine?　Gems from the sea-caves?　Or a lamb from the flock?

SHEPHERDS.

Gold we have not, and myrrh we have none, nor odors, nor pearls; and we bethought not a lamb.

God guided your thoughts. Ye simple and guileless, pass on !'
God guided your thoughts. He is your lamb ; the Babe whom ye
seek.

SHEPHERDS.

His angel said, Go ; and, lo ! we go ; bearing our crooks,
bearing our staves, bearing our reeds, to sing at His feet.

Your reeds, and your prayers. Ye favored of Heaven, the ages
shall grow, and his saints at the Christmas-tides sing :

> " Vainly with gifts would we His favor secure,
>   Richer by far is the heart's adoration,
>   Dearer to God are the prayers of the poor."

And ye come first. His poor. " Blessed are the poor." His
poor. " Not many rich." " Not many great." The poor come
first with sandals wet with dew.

> And they never turned aside
> (Did an unseen angel guide ?) [3]
> Till they reached the sacred manger,
> Till they found the Heavenly Stranger.

PART II.

ADORATION.

Cold on His cradle the dew-drops are shining,
  Low lies His head with the beasts of the stall ;
Angels adore Him in slumber reclining,
  Maker and Monarch and Saviour of all.
                                    BISHOP HEBER.

And they ?   Gaze in a sweet amaze, and pray as comprehend-
ing nought, save it is blessed to be there, and Heaven's gate ; and
they, godly, devout, life-long, had never seemed before to pray, to
talk with very God ; and morn surprised them on their knees, and
then, when they arose and went back to their flocks and care ; there
is a sermon sure in that; also in that they told to all the region
round about the angel-visit of, and how they in the manger sought
the Babe, and found what marvellous young child.   Moreover, how
the people heard and marvelled at their words ; and Mary, blessed,
all these doings pondered in her heart.   A sermon writ in each we
find, or poem sweet, or both ; and, written o'er the face of all, how
God develops clear beyond all doubt; yet touches with development the human mind to only gradual take His great truths in.

PART III.

" Solem ambo pariunt Aurora et Virgo ; sed ista
Solem viva parit ; dum parit illa, perit." [4]

O, blessed night !   O, sweetest morn ! an ancient poet on it looked and sang, " The vines of Engaddi fresh blossomed that night," and
I had once my dream before I read that poem in a line.   A dream
almost as brief, and unto me with whom 'twas born, almost as
sweet: and that, my actual dream, took on my mind such actual
hold, I counted it erewhile as like to a tradition somewhere read.
The dream of which I tell : Aurora breathed upon the clouds, and it
was morn, first Christmas morn.   Sweet Virgin, Mary-mother, step-

ped from out the cave to show her babe a morn of earth, and morn
her babe—when lo, she saw a new flower on the earth—a flower
born on that night, and blooming close unto the manger-door—we
call it *Star of Bethlehem*, e'er-since.

CHAPTER IV.

EIGHT DAYS OLD.

LUKE ii. 21.

TEARS in thy eyes, young mother! Wherefore? Ay,
'Tis the first time thou hast missed the darling Babe,
For eight sweet mornings pillowed on thy breast.
The law of circumcision claims its due,
And thou must yield thy sinless first-born up.
Canst thou not miss Him for a time so brief;
Not give *Him* up to the first taste of pain,
Who 'twixt the law and mortals yet must stand;
Oh, mother, over-fond; nor weep to wait ;
Nay, thy young mother-love is tender yet
As budding amaranth that days of sun
And nights of dew must ripen into bloom
The sturdy flower no after winds may blight.
And His, the sensitive, the sacred flesh,
The unmarred, moulded beauty, fresh from God,
Yea, thou mayest weep ; and yet weep soft, for thou,

Princess of Judah, in thy manger-bed
Hast known a joy, the queenliest sovereign
With a kingdom's heir asleep upon her arm,
Ne'er knew.　The chamber where the rustling silk
Shrouds with its gorgeous folds the regal couch,
Bowered ne'er a mother and a babe so fair.
And this, thy past week, hath the sweetest been,
In all thy young life's richly radiant hours.
This trial sharp, the first grief-shadow casts,
And tearfully thy eyes turn toward the door
Through which good Joseph bore thy Babe ;
For thee, the glory all went out with Him.
To share with Him, and thy heart followed close,
Nor waiteth long, the listening head low-bent,
For first wail of thy infant dear, it comes :
The eyes that plead for Him, dear Babe ! behold ;
The pining arms outstretched, infold : and He,
Nestled like wounded dove unto thy breast,
The comfort finds nature and mothers give
Their babes.

CHAPTER V.

PRESENTATION-MORN.

PART I.

"It was a glorious temple ! . . . .
  Scarce might the gazer's dazzled eye repose,
  For gold and gems around its walls did fling
  A wondrous lustre—columns glittering
Crowned with fair chaplets raised the roof on high,
  And in the Oracle the gilded wing
  Of Cherubim veiled in deep mystery
The sacred ark in which the law of God doth lie."

MORIAH'S fair and queenly brow uplifts,
    Magnificent in beauty, temple-crowned,[5]
Like some bold Alpine peak amid whose robe
Of diamond snows the beams of morning play.
The temple of the Jews ! O, it was grand !
Stately and grand ! pre-eminent and proud !
Nor earth had other such.   Vast marble walls
And roof of snowy stone, where sunrise poured
Till all the molten spikes that round about
The golden eavings edged, girt like a fringe
Of flame the dazzling white.
                     'Sunrise and prayer !'
The golden trumpets sound, and multitudes
Troop to the call, phylacteried Jew and priest,

And Zion's temple looms amid the smoke
Of morning sacrifice.

               Two worshippers
Wend up the holy hill, sweetly sedate;
Sedate and slow; Shiloh's bright brook flows near;
Jerusalem, "*Joy of the earth,*" unrolled
Like a fair map in beauty at their feet,
The glory of the Lebanons afar;
Haste maketh waste in worship or in love;
The hand that lingers in its tender clasp,
The lips that pause within their kiss to breathe,
The feet that reverent to the altar near,
Yea, every passion pure at fullest flow,
As waters deep, slow moves, gathering each thrill
Of sweetness in its move; slowly they come,
Reverent the broad ascending steps they climb:
A babe of beauty marvellous, the man
Bears tenderly, his sinewy arms within,
And she who by him walks in modest veil,
A little willow basket on her arm
Twin turtles hold.

               Beneath the golden vine
That shadows bright the sacred door they pause.
O, picture chaste, and rich, and beautiful!
Methinks I at the Gate of Beauty stand.
Along the colonnade of pillars grand,

Massive and high of polished porphyry
Inlaid with pearl and lavish veined with gold,
My kindling vision sweeps the vista broad
And rests on them beneath the golden grape.

PART II.

"Lift up your heads, ye gates o'erlaid with gold,
For lo, the King of Glory enters there!"

SCENE—*An ante-chamber of the Temple, Joseph and Mary in the midst of the floor, waiting, momentarily waiting, for what they divine not—waiting.*

Who is he that cometh up through the deep porches beyond, over across the floor of ivory and fir, within the House of Cedars? Who is he that cometh with locks white for the reaper? Who is he that cometh with tottering step, quickened, yet grandly, swiftly reverent, a patriarch making haste slowly? Who is he that cometh? It is aged Simeon, drawn by the Spirit in. And who is aged Simeon drawn by the Spirit in?

The aged Simeon, a man devout,
The man for Israel's consolation,
The consolation waiting long that lies
In Mary's arms.   Dear Babe of Consolation!
Waited for long—long for, by that good man,
Outliving for this hope his span of years.
"He must be good!"   Look up into his eyes,
His prophet-eyes, see how they glow!   The man
It is—th' man with whom the Holy Ghost talks!

Talks at the eve—talks in the silent night!
The Holy Ghost has told him of this child,
Has promised him the sight, and lo, he comes,
Drawn by the Spirit in, his palsied hands outstretched.
Dear, good, old, glorious Simeon! looking
Into the bright Babe's eyes; beautiful eyes!
"Now hath mine eyes thy full salvation seen!"
Folding—folding the bright Babe to his heart,
"Lord, let thy servant now in peace depart!"
And Simeon blessèd them—the holy three.
Placing the bright Babe in His mother's arms,
Was it a tear upon the sweet babe-lids?
Was it the look on the face of the Babe,
Looking back—back to his face for pity,
Pity for the woe he had come to take;
Or yet, red spots mid the curls where the thorns
Must pierce, he saw—and looking sadly down
The paschal-way, the shadow of a cross?
Giving the Babe to the arms of the mother,
"And a sword through thine own soul."
———————————————————*O Mater !*
"*Mater dolorosa!*" Woman transfixed!
Gazing with Simeon down the paschal-way,
"Mother of Sorrows," thy heart absorbs a pain
That will not go till thou shalt stand assumed
In heaven.

PART III.

> " Then came an aged prophetess, whose days
> Were spent in fastings and in ceaseless prayer
> Within the temple   .   .   .   .   .
> Rejoice ye aged, who in patience bear
> Your burden, for on you the blessing lies,
> From youth withheld, and God's most gracious care
> Strengthened the feeble knees, and fading eyes
> Saw through their misty veil the Morning Star arise."

The pious prophetess of Israel comes,

Girt with the sackcloth and the sable veil,

From solemn fast 'neath God's high altar-shade,

And of that child prophetic speaks to those

Who for redemption look, and wait, and pray.

Thus Anna's faith brings balm for Simeon's sword.

PART IV.

SCENE—*Going in unto the altar of immolation, Joseph and Mary bearing her babe, Simeon and Anna attending.*

> " The prophet's warning unforgot,
> Shading her soul's fond hope—yet quenching not ;
> For not the mother who her infant brings
> To fountains where baptismal waters flow,
> Can know the joy that in her bosom springs
> Who to God's altar bears the King of kings."

Where Zion's white-robed priests

With smoking censers round their altars bow,

Thrice-sweetly solemn that pure mother lays

Her first-born on the altar down.   Herself

5

The priest, oblates Him in her heart to God ;
Silent adores Him there as sacrifice,
And God—then buys Him back with offering brought
And placed with meekness in the priestly hand ;
A throb of pity in her tender breast
E'en for the timid doves that die for Him :
Oh, mother kind, too poor to bring a lamb ;
Knows she what lamb her arms infold ?

———◆———

CHAPTER VI.

NAZARETH.

"TO THEIR OWN CITY NAZARETH."—LUKE ii. 39.

Not far from Mount Carmel of the high sycamores and black firs, coming down the declivities of Hermon, descending into a vale, " green oaks, myrtles, vines, and olives " abound ; " fields of barley, wheat, and trefoil " are putting forth their green spears ; Adar, month of warm winds, has come with the singing of birds. From time to time " an isolated castle perched on the craggy point of a rock overhangs the roadside," and ever and anon " opulent villages peep through colonnades of palms ; " " men in garments of goats' hair "—" women enveloped in purple cloaks and wearing white veils " going in and out at the gates. This cool vale, within a dark border of high mountains, is the valley of Esdraelon ; at the extremity of which appears a little town picturesquely " situated on a hillside, shining like a rare flower in the midst of the surrounding hamlets "—Nazareth, by interpretation, " City of Flow-

ers;" Nazareth, the birthplace of the "Fair Rose of Jericho."
Who are these coming down the mountains of Hermon, up through
this vale of Esdraelon, up to this Nazareth?   A man and a woman;
a babe in the arms of the woman, and the woman riding a snow-
white mule.   This man, venerable and tall, "the joy of the elect
diffused over his face," "a statue in whom all perfections shine."
This woman, so beautiful as to dazzle the sight!⁶   The mystical
moon that Solomon saw; deriving her splendor from the Sun in her
arms.   This Babe—Jesus Christ, the young Jesus Christ—the ever-
radiant Sun, who inundated her with his brightness before he came
into the world.   This woman, the Mystical Rose in the poets of
Sion; the Mystical Rose in the garden of Paradise; the Mystical
Rose, deriving all her odors of holiness from the Bud in her arms,
the ever-resplendent Flower that irradiated her with His beauty
before He was born; that perfumed her with His fragrance before
He appeared upon the earth.   This venerable man, this glorious
woman; this Mystery of God in babehood; Jesus, Mary, Joseph—
the three marvellous lights of the world; "the three golden lilies
of the Universe" are these, coming up to Nazareth, coming home
unto Nazareth.   Home unto Nazareth! Ave Nazareth! Ave Nazareth!   The daughter of Nazareth cometh to her home, bearing her
child!   Child begotten in Nazareth, born in Bethlehem, consecrated
at Jerusalem, borne back to be cradled in thee, blessed Nazareth!
Cradle of the Christ!   Ave Nazareth!   Blessed Nazareth!

CHAPTER VII.

THE THREE KINGS OF THE ORIENT.

"THERE CAME WISE MEN FROM THE EAST."—MATT. ii.
"HE SHALL LIVE, AND UNTO HIM SHALL BE GIVEN OF THE GOLD OF ARABIA."—"THE KINGS OF ARABIA AND SABA SHALL BRING GIFTS."—PSALM lxxii.

PART I.

We three kings of Orient are
Bearing gifts ; we traverse afar
Field and fountain,
Moor and mountain,
Following yonder star.

Star of wonder, Star of Night,
Star with royal beauty bright,
Westward leading,
Still proceeding,
Guide us to thy perfect light.

Rev. J. H. HOPKINS, Jr.

And, the star disappearing, they came up to Jerusalem, saying, at the capitol, and the temple, shall we not find the child ?

'TIS a festal hour in Herod's hall,
And the dancers' feet in cadence fall
With the joyous notes of a harper-band
Who strike each string with a cunning hand,
Till the captured eye dilates with whirls,
And follows entranced those dancing girls

Whose flying feet a chorus swells—
The silver ring of their ankle bells.
Not the gossamer robe with its flowing fold,
Not the zoning girdle of woven gold,
Not the gems that shine in their sable hair,
But those white arms flung to the perfumed air,
And the mocking glance of the starry eye
Draws from the courtier train a sigh.
On, on they dance in the choral ring,
Anon in the mimic chase they spring,
Till the panting breath each rose-lip cleaves,
And the bodiced bosom wildly heaves :
Then in labyrinth maze the footsteps grow
With the softened harp-tone-sigh more slow,
And quavering poised with the dying note,
The fairy dancers cease to float.

Again the silver bowls are crowned,
And the thirsty lip in the red wine drowned ;
And the tide of the royal mirth flows clear,
Till a herald bold the throne stalks near,
Seeking an heir to the Jewish throne,
Whose regal star [7] in the East hath shone.

HEROD.

' An heir to the throne ! star in the East ! '
Gods ! what a shock breaks in on the feast !
' In with the guests, whose face we'd know !
Woe unto whom false marvels show ! '

SCENE—*Herod and his Court, the three kingly Magi on the right of the throne ; a pompous train in the rear.*

'Twas an august band in the banquet hall,
The kings of the East, who came at call ;
'Twas an august sight in the regal hall,
When the desert king strode at the haughty call
To the very foot of the pompous throne,
And towered up there in his grandeur alone,
Stately and tall—some fourscore nigh—
With the flash that awes in his princely eye.
O'er his dark robe wrought with stars of gold,
The silver beard to his girdle rolled ;
The hieroglyphical, seer-charmed wand,
Like a sceptre swayed in a kingly hand ;
He stood (and the awe crept through the regal room)
'Twixt the throne and revel like an angel of doom.

HEROD (*recovering*).

Ho, kings of the Orient ! what of your land ?
What of your visions, and what of our hand ?

MELCHIOR.

We honor thy ripe locks![8]   Long life, O sire !
Thy servants from the Orient's generous heart !
Our gifts, offspring of womb prolific
In all like wisdom and virtue odorous,
And shining, have breaths of th' frankincense shades,
And ' tears of Paradise '[9] smelt 'mid the sands
That never lose the earnest of the sun ;
Where, at her tent-door, every desert-maid
Watches the rising of her own fair star,
And Ishmael's wildest wandering son reads out
The hour by orbs that all night come and go,
Bright sentinels ! each at his shining post,
To watch the ways of men, and record them above !

(Herod winces.)

We from our youth have pale Arcturus known,
Traced the Bear's circles round the Northern Pole,
Drank from the quenchless light-tide flowing bright
And constant from the Dipper's star-wrought bowl,
Counted the gems in Orion's studded belt,
And tracked the Serpent's windings vast,
Earth interlacing in his shining coils,
Followed each planet's course, and loved like nought
Of earth, the twinkling handmaids of the night :
Such is our land,[10] and such, O king, are we.[11]

Herod.

The star! Of the star of the augury? What, and
when?

Melchior.

When last the full moon in the zenith rode,
We stood, our plain within, the night to read.
  " Never had been a night,
  Never was since a night,
  Never will be a night
  Like it forever ! " [12]

O, night so full of mystery and light !
O, night so luminous with largened stars !
When suddenly the East grew yet a-glow,
And upward sailed, a silver cloud upon,
A star, new-born, from out whose dazzling points
Gushed light ineffable.

  O, star effulgent !
  Brilliantly beautiful !
  Gorgeously glorious !
  Sun-like and king-like and God-like !

Each golden constellation wheeled in heaven,
And every planet in the azure tracts afar,
With sphere-born melody rolled near and swept

With tread of music-motion in its train,
When as a prince the armied host it led,

> The king-star of wonder,
> The king-star of splendor,
> " Glowed till outglowing
> Every star in the heavens."

GASPARD AND BALTHAZAR.

Magnificently marvellous,
Beckoned us on to follow !

MELCHIOR.

Lo, we have come!
Where is the Heir,
The Prince and the Saviour,
The Desire of the nations we seek ?

THREE KINGS (*in chorus*).

Lo, in the East His star we have seen,
King of the Jews where is He that is born?

PART II.

"AND HEROD WAS TROUBLED."

"AND HEROD WAS TROUBLED, AND ALL JERUSALEM WITH HIM."

SCENE—*Herod's hall, the priesthood entering*

Chief of the Jews, phylacteried Pharisee,
Each Rabbi holding close his breath of dread.

HEROD.

Doctors of Moses and the Law, the Christ!
Where shall be born, the Christ?

                There is a gleam!
Out-struck as torch-light by an ill wind flared;
Woe-tide!   There still is one remembered here;
For beauty, grace, for loftiness, all hearts
He held!   Betrayed to death!   'His crime?'   Of
    blood!
A kingly race, a throne the priesthood barred;
He died![13]   'How?'   Herod knew.   Ay, at this hour
The beauteous Mariamne's[14] injured ghost
Uprises at her murderous husband's side,
With their two headless sons![15]   Oh, dead rebuke!
Oh, evil hour and rule for hopeful birth!

Grim-visaged war, with gory fillets bound,
Stirs at the call!   Faint answer comes : Thus saith
The prophet of the Lord, " In Bethlehem."

PART III.

SCENE—*Herod giving banquet to the Kings.*

The fragrant spice-lamps shower the regal board,
And Herod quaffs with smile; bright opes the feast,
Bright flow the music and the wine.   The wine
Is old and mellow fire.   The king is bland
To-night.

HEROD.

A draught! cup-bearer of our heart!

(In the rich flare of golden floodings ringed
The flattered satrap lifts the jewelled bowl,
And Herod quaffs ' A crown unto the king new-born!'
The wine is old and mellow fire.   The king
Is bland to-night.)

HEROD.

' The royal vassalage!'
Aside. (An heir, who comes to king it over all,
We'll see them greedy drink with pious faith.)

Low at the star-seers' feet bent courtierly
The graceful bearer of the kingly pledge,
The rich, red grape a-glitter with the bead,
Nor Herod's cup, our desert-kings ensnare.

GASPARD.

Bear back unlipped, our pledge.   Pardon, O king,
But royal sire, our fathers drank not wine.[16]

HEROD (*aside.*)

Gods! and the conquering bowl takes not.   What next?
'Tis wine—not Herod, that is foiled to-night.
Once there was honey in our tongue, and oil
Of winning words.   Back wine!   We take the lists.

(Where the voluptuous cushions pillowed lie
In regal beauty piled the alabaster urn
Burns low; the revellers drop off as leaves
From some red, passionate flower that hath been
" Intemperate with the sun."   One eunuch grim
And four kings left.)

HEROD.

                Before we part, the hour!
Fathers and kings! the magic hour, when first

Ye favored saw the king-star rise. Go, now,
Search ye with diligence, search well;
Search till the kingly heir is haply found.
We envy ye, ye lead the way; but lead;
Our gifts impatient wait. When first ye find,
Return, and we may worship at such feet.

PART IV.

Through the lordly palace-gate
    Swept a gorgeous camel-train,
Slowly through the wondering street
    Winding toward the distant plain,
Swept the kingly cavalcade, Eastern, regal, bright,
    Straight toward Bethlehem [17] had turned;
        But the re-appearing star
    On its throne of silver-cloud,
        Beamed upon them not afar,
Beamed upon them, and they paused, as the tender light
        Of the sweet star lit and shone;
        Praised the God of kings most High;
        Praised him for the kingly birth,
            And His herald in the sky,
Brighter growing, brighter than the fairest star of night!
        Praised, as they praised, from the star
            Circling o'er each bowèd head,

Fell a halo, and they turned;
    Close to follow where it led,
Pressed the star-led cavalcade, radiant star in sight.
    Straight as Israel's cloudy pillar
        Led the Hebrew host by day,
    And by night, transfused to fire,
        Tracked the pathless desert-way,
Led the star of " royal beauty," Herald of the Infinite,
    Till it hovered o'er the cot,
    Goldened o'er the sacred spot
    Where they heard the Holy Maid
    Singing to her Blessed Babe.

MARY (singing.)

Sleep, my Angel-Birdling, sleep,
    Bow thy blessèd head to rest,
Thou wilt find no softer pillow,
    Darling, than a mother's breast;
Angel-Birdling, sleep caressed,
Lovingly upon my breast.

I will watch the rose-lid curtain
    Veiling o'er the God-lit eyes,
Till the soft and shadowy fringe,
    Sleeping on the pearl-cheek lies;

O, what bliss such watch to keep !
Babe, beloved, sweetly sleep.

Beautiful, O child, is earth,
   Roofed with rays of golden light,
Circled round with singing waves
   Velvety with verdure bright,
Sprinkled with an angel-thought
In each colored flower-bell wrought.

Beautiful ! and yet my only,
   There is nought so fair to me,
Azure heaven and emerald earth
   Wears no other gem like Thee !
Sweetest gift of Father-love,
Sleep, my tender Angel-Dove.

When the sweet-breathed morning wakes,
   When the vesper-shadows grow,
Does my Loved One never hear
   Angel-footsteps come and go ?
See'st not o'er Thy lovely head,
Gleam of seraph-wing outspread ?

Sleep, then, Angel-Birdling, sleep,
   Fondly folded here to rest ;

Thou wilt find no softer pillow,
   Darling, than a mother's breast :
Angel-Birdling, sleep caressed,
Lovingly upon my breast.

PICTURE.

(Before the holy house of Nazareth.)

Star of the East,
Over the thatch of yellow moss ;
Over the threshold,
Over the sward,
Over the kings
(Long-bearded magi
From the Orient afar),
Over the camels in rear,
Over all,
Falls the glow of the star ;
Richly magnificent,
Softly resplendent,
Falls the glow of the star.
Falls the glow goldenly
Over the cot,
Falls the glow crimsonly
Over the turf,
Goldenly, crimsonly,
Over the cot, over the turf.

O, it was beautiful!
The star, the cot, and the turf.
O, it was worshipful!
The singing that drifted in sweetness
From within to without;
Beautiful! worshipful! soulful!

And they held their very breath,
Silent as the pulse of death,
Till the sweet ethereal lay
Melted in the air away,
Then with foot unsandalled, bare,
With uncovered, hoary hair,
Reverent crossed the corridor,
Stood entranced upon the floor,
All their soul with wonder laden,
Gazing on that Blessed Maiden,
On whose velvet bosom lay
Loveliest born of human clay.

Low they bowed with adoration,
Laid with words of rapt devotion,
Judah's Princely Babe to greet,
Costly offerings at His feet.
Treasures rich from Orient lands,
Gold-dust bright from Afric's sands,

Radiant gems whose rainbow blaze
Kindled 'neath a tropic's rays,
Odorous myrrh and spices sweet,
Laid with worship at His feet.

O Mary, rich Mary, with the gems and the gold,
Ablaze at thy beauteous feet !
She heedeth them not, the treasures untold,
Nor the breath of the incense sweet ;
She sees but the worship, the heart-worship piled
At the sacred feet of her sacred Child.
With her God on her breast,
How can she be made rich ?   He who hath God, hath
all ;
Equal the palace, equal the stall ;
He is her incense, He is her gold,
Her myrrh and her jewels, and her all.

O'er that maiden-mother fair,
Clasping all so sweet her care,
Lulled within her charmed caress,
Babe the Orient princes bless,
Woman glorified and mild,
Jesse's maid and Jesse's child,
Radiant with incarnate charms
Throned in her loving arms ;

> O'er those magi bowed so lowly,
> Lost in adorations holy—
> Sacred tableau ; angels smiled,
> Smiled, and stepped from out the sky,
> In the mid-air hovered nigh.

O wondering angels ! O happy kings ! O blessed mother ! O beautiful young Saviour-child ! Let us worship, too, and leave our hearts at Thy feet.

NOTES TO BOOK III.

1. BETHLEHEM, by interpretation, " City of Bread," also called Bethlehem of Juda, to distinguish it from Bethlehem in the province of the tribe of Zebulon, was about eight leagues distant from Jerusalem. Michaes calls it Ephrata, from the name of the mother of its founder.

2. " At the foot of stony Bethlehem is a stable cut in the rock, with its crib, for the use of beasts of burden, and there it is that the Incarnate Word was born."—JEROME, in his 108th *Letter to Eustochium.*

3. There is a tradition that the shepherds heard the angels sing, and were thus guided unto the holy manger. Luke says, an angel was sent to tell the shepherds ; and Matthew, that a star appeared to the wise men.

4. " The sun is born of the dawn, but the dawn dies in giving birth to the sun. Jesus is born of Mary ; but at the birth of Jesus, Mary receives a fairer life."

5. High above all, on a precipitous rock, rose the temple, fortified and adorned by Solomon. The temple was as strong without as a citadel, within more adorned than a palace. On entering you beheld porticoes of numberless columns of porphyry, marble, and alabaster ;

gates adorned with gold and silver, among which was the wonderful gate called the Beautiful. Farther on, through the vast arch, was the sacred portal which admitted into the interior of the temple itself, all sheeted over with gold, and overhung by a vine-tree of gold, the branches of which were as large as a man. The roof of the temple, even on the outside, was set over with golden spikes, to prevent the birds settling there. At a distance, the whole temple looked like a mountain of snow, fretted with golden pinnacles.—*From Titus's Letter.*

6. Joseph was a statue in which shone all perfection.—EUSEBIUS. St. Dyonesus, who had seen her (the Blessed Virgin), says "she was so beautiful as to dazzle the sight, and he would have adored her as a goddess had he not known there was only one God."

7. Aburfarage says (*Historia Dynastiarum*) : "Zerdaschet predicted to the magi the birth of the Messiah, born of a virgin, and that at the time of his birth a strange star appeared, which conducted them to the place, and ordained them to bear presents."—*Vide* note 3, Chap. II., Book I.

8. Herod died at the age of seventy, of a horrible malady, soon after the massacre of the babes of Bethlehem.

9. The Arabians call gold the tears of Allah.

10. Cyril, Basil, and others maintain the magi came from Persia, and others from Chaldea, Mesopotamia, and India. James of Ausole says: "They were no others than Enoch, Melchizedek, and Elias, come from the earthly paradise to visit the Messias in his cradle; but the most received opinion is that they came from Arabia."

11. Bede thus describes them (*in Collect*) : "First, Melchior, old and pale, with long beard and hair, who offered gold to the Lord; second, Gaspard, young, beardless, ruddy, who offered incense, an oblation worthy of a God; third, Balthazar, a Moor, with a long beard: ·he offered myrrh, which signified that the Son of Man was to die." Ancient paintings represent them crowned with Phrygian mitres.

Regem Deumque annunciant
Thesaurus et fragrans odor
Thuris Sabæi ac myrrhæus
Pulvis sepulchrum prædocet.

> Offerings of mystic meaning!
> Incense doth the God disclose;
> Gold a royal child proclaimeth,
> Myrrh a future tomb foreshows.
>
> *Lauds of the Epiphany.*

12. " Never had been a night," &c.
" Glowed till out-glowing."
From Ellida, a Poem, by Rev. H. H. Saunderson.

13. Herod, the distinguished warrior-prince of the Idumean line, married with Mariamni, the adored princess of Asmonean descent, whose line was in highest repute among the Jews, and made Aristobulus, her brother, who with his sister were the only representatives of the Asmonean house, high-priest. The Jewish priesthood and crown could never be united, and permanent peace between the warring factions seemed secured. But the jealousy of Herod being awakened by the greater love of the people for their priest, Aristobulus was invited to an evening bath by his brother-in-law, where, the lights being suddenly extinguished, he was strangled in the darkness by the king's emissary.

14. Mariamni (whose story Grace Aguillar tells with beautiful pathos, her magnificence of beauty and sweetness, her devotion to her only brother, her conjugal devotion and wrongs) the malign assassination at once and irrevocably alienated in affections. Herod, stung to madness by the passive allegiance of the wife and queen, immovable in the loftiness of her quiet sorrow and rebuke, and wrought upon by his mother and sister, Salome, haters of the Asmonean blood, in the paroxysms of unrequited love, and jealous of her better right to the throne, sent his young and high-minded queen, in the very flower of her beauty, to the block, and, haunted by remorse, for two years after, wandered like a maniac abroad. See also Byron's poem, *Mariamni*.

15. By Mariamni, Herod had two sons, who were brought up at Rome. Polished and highly educated, these young princes returned to their father's court, when, again stirred by hatred of the rival blood that mingled in their veins, he provoked a quarrel, and sent both to the scaffold. Would he who had spared neither queen-wife nor son, abdicate for their young Messiah? And all Jerusalem was troubled.

16. *Vide* Jeremiah : descendants of the Rechabites.

17. Tradition locates the holy family at Bethlehem during the visit of the wise men. In accordance with the Mosaic law, Mary could not leave the city till the days of her purification were accomplished, when she went up to the temple to fulfil the obligation of a mother in Israel for her first-born. Different doctors try to find a reason for her turning aside on her way home to Nazareth, very inconvenient to account for. Was it to visit and adore the sacred birthplace again, before she should go down to her home? She had, as it were, just come up from thence, and He who made Bethlehem holy was in her very arms, flooding every avenue of her heart with reverence, worship, and affection. With the Christ-Babe in her bosom, folded with full satisfaction to her heart, how could she want to go anywhere for adoration? Was not all embraced in her arms, gathered to her bosom? Meanwhile the Scripture records seem of themselves explicit : "The shepherds," not wise men, came, as Luke writes, "and found the young child, with Mary his mother and Joseph, lying in the manger. The child being eight days old was circumcised, and a month (or forty days) old, was presented in the temple at Jerusalem, after which they returned to their own city Nazareth." (Luke ii. 32.) Where probably the magi, or wise men, described by Matthew, were led by the re-appearing star; re-appearing that they might not turn aside to Bethlehem. Thus Herod, deceived by the prophecy as to their residence, commenced the slaughter of the Holy Innocents at Bethlehem, while the holy family were yet in Nazareth. Thus the wise men had time to make their journey from the far East, with camels, and the slow movements of a dignified and royal cavalcade on a journey of peace, a visit of holy congratulation and worship.

BOOK IV.

OR

BOOK OF THE EXILE.

THERE is the sunset in the wilderness, the great orb flashing on the rim of the desert-horizon, its light reflected in Joseph's eyes ; and then there is Jesus sleeping on His Mother's lap, and the round moon above, and the glittering well, and the whispering palm, and the night breathing heavily over the yellow sands.—FABER.

CONTENTS.

CHAPTER I.

FLIGHT.

AND BEING WARNED OF GOD IN A DREAM THAT THEY SHOULD NOT RE-
TURN UNTO HEROD, THEY DEPARTED UNTO THEIR COUNTRY ANOTHER WAY.
AND WHEN THEY WERE DEPARTED, BEHOLD, THE ANGEL OF THE LORD AP-
PEARETH TO JOSEPH IN A DREAM.—MATT. ii.

SCENE—*Joseph by the couch of the Virgin and Child, having just
related the vision of the Angel.*

THEN rose that tender mother up,
　　Up with her perilled child,
With fainting pulse and cold heart-beat
　　And sudden tremor wild.

But Joseph as he careful wraps
　　The Babe upon his arm,
Speaks of the safety and the trust
　　In Him who shields from harm.

The angel of his warning dream
　　Seems lingering with him still;
Thus calm he girts the saddled mule,
　　The sacks for journey fill;

Thus calm he speaks his trembling spouse,
  ' Bear forth the timely gold;
And now thy hood and mantle, dear,
  Around thee closer fold.'

Out through the silent gates they pass
  Ere yet the city wakes;
Still at the watchman's drowsy call
  The timid mother quakes.

'Tis only when they joyful trace
  The rugged mountain-track,
She ceases first to frequent turn
  With glance of terror back;

First dares to lift her shrouding veil
  To kiss her rescued Child,
And drink her rapture from the eyes
  That upward beam so mild.

Hark! Rachel's wail comes up the glen;
  O, tender mother fly!
The sword is out! a thousand babes
  In Bethlehem-region die.

CHAPTER II.

AMONG THE MOUNTAINS.

BE THOU LIKE A ROE OR A YOUNG HART AMONG THE MOUNTAINS.—CANT.

PART I.

BURSHEBA.

CAUTIOUS and slow among the mountains wild,
 Threading, with feet like fugitives, by-paths
And ways remote, they come, till weariedly
The cliffs are scaled, and through the rocky throat
Of Hazernal they climb.
      Gone is their store,
The barley loaf and figs, the bottled wine,
But rest by Bursheba's sweet well is good,
And meekest Mary sits beneath a date
That spreads its fruitless boughs the well above,
Dips her warm brow and parched lips in the waves,
Thanks God for living springs, and asks of Him
In His own good time to send them food;
And next with modest grace affectionate,
Down-kneels to wash the tired and dusty feet
Of him who all the weary days, patient,
A-foot, had goaded on the jaded mule;
Then turned unto the barren tree where she

Had laid her Babe, asleep, she joyful saw
The waving boughs, the young Child's bed above,
Just o'er His head, with ripe fruit-clusters thick.[1]

PART II.

MARTYR-BABES OF BETHLEHEM.

> Lovely flower of martyrs, hail,
> Smitten by the tyrant foe
> On life's threshold, as the gale
> Strews the roses ere they blow
>   PRUDENTIUS.

Day dies the crimsoned occident within,
By Abram's sacred well our travellers sleep.

O, there is no hour like evening
  In an Orient summer-time,
When the golden moon and stars
  Up the azure zenith climb ;
When earth's panting bosom cools
  'Neath the soft baptismal dews,
When all toil and sin and strife
  Hallowed nature seems to lose ;
When the choir of drowsy birds
  Tire of the warbled number,
When the nodding palms are sleepy,
  When the flower-buds droop with slumber ;

O, there is no hour like evening
   In an Orient summer-time,
When a golden moon and stars
   Up the azure zenith climb
To shining walk the broad blue floor of heaven,
And a paradise-like calm comes to crown the lighted even;
Dew to earth, sleep to man, dreams and rest and peace
   fresh given.

Such the hour, balmy, holy,
   Sweetly sleeping, babe in-armed,
Mary-mother sees in dreaming,
   Hover softly round encharmed,
Lo, a band of infant cherubs, bending o'er her lowly bed,
From their crowns a starry brightness over all the sleepers
   shed.

How their white wings o'er her couch
   Rustle with a joyful sound;
How they bend in awe and wonder,
   How they brightly circle round!
One celestial draweth nearer, .
   And a cherub-accent clear
Thrills the maiden-mother's heart,
   Ringeth in her charmèd ear:

ANGEL.

Angel-sister ! angel-brother !
　　See the Christ Babe sleeping here !
Know Him by the haloed head !
　　Know Him by the tender tear !
We will bide the laggard dawning
　　For a look within the eyes
Of the Babe all heaven adoreth,
　　Babe beloved in the skies.
Bud of Jesse !　Sharon's Rose !　God-like human flower !
Maid of Israel, in and 'round thy heaven-like bower,
　　　'Tis a charge the angels crave
　　　　Thus to guard thy sacred bed ;
　　　'Tis a charge the angels love
　　　　Thus to shield thy blessèd head :
Heaven is where the Incarnate and His tender mother
　　　dwell ;
Gaze ye down upon them, seraphs ; sweeter let your an-
　　　thems swell.

　　　We were the first martyrs for him,[2]
　　　　We the babes that Herod slew,
　　　When the wail of Rama piercèd
　　　　Through the holy heavens blue :
　　　Thus we won the tender guerdon,
　　　　Holiest angels sweetest prize,

Here to watch while soft-dewed slumber
Seals His mother's loving eyes.
Sleep, then, tranquil mother, sleep, though midnight darken ;
'Round thy bower His angels stay to hearken.

We have knelt beside that river
On its golden-sanded shore,
In whose life-wave flows a draught
He who quaffs shall thirst no more ;
As it will e'er yet be written in the Mystic Word.
We have plucked the flowers that spring
Fresh from an immortal sod,
Stood beneath the fruitful tree
In the Paradise of God,
Seen the splendors of the City of the Lord ;
But our bosoms glow more sweetly
Gazing on thy Babe of Heaven ;
O, it was our life's rich moment,
When our life for His was given,
Paradise and palms for one stroke of Herod's sword.

Sleep, the breezes blow but balm ;
Sleep, the midnight skies are calm ;
While the dewy hours cast diamonds
On yon grove of flowering almonds,

6*

Dews shall fall on almond's head,
Not around thy haloed bed.
Through the fragrant boughs soft numbers
Angels hum to lull thy slumbers,
Bright the seraph wings above
Canopy thy couch of love :
Sleep, the stars above thee shine,
But brighter o'er the bed divine;
Babe of a celestial birth,
Woman on the fragrant turf,
Prostrate manhood slumbering nigh,
Helpless now with closèd eye,
E'en thou wearied beast at rest,
Sleep, ye all are guarded, blest.

PART III.

THE LEPER BOY;

OR,

Morning—Before the Noon—Noon—Afternoon—Night.

MORN.

While the gold and the rose, in-blushed with the blue,
Are tender a-glow o'er the brows of the mountains,
Dew-beaming, reaching up to sky-brightness,
Glorious old mountains, olden and Orient,

Fetlock deep in the dewy thyme,
Jogs on the famed ancient mule,
The snow-white mule, Elabothania,
Mary-maid, sweet Mother-maid,
Bearing her Babe afar to the Egypt-land.

The antelope looks down from his craggy height,
The sky-cleaving eagle from his eyrie mounts up,
And the cony shies 'neath the firs as they pass,
Our three, journeying on to the Egypt-land.

BEFÓRE THE NOON.

A growing bloom on the foot-tracks left behind,
A hum of the bees where the flowers thicken.

NOON.

Under the cedars,
Nested with care in the golden gorse,
Cradled in moss the Christ-Child sleeps.

JOSEPH (*adoring*).

O, beautiful child! Herod can never harm Thee!
O, marvellous child! Herod can never slay Thee!
Babe of a Virgin!   Babe of God!   God-Babe!
He who watches Israel never slumbers!
His angel spake, and we flee!

Mary-Mother (*gathering in a cup honey that drips
from the rocks*).

Dates last night, honey to day ; God careth
For us—for love of His Son !   Blessed Son !

AFTERNOON.

JOSEPH.

Northward, lo !   Is it a bird in the sky ?

MARY.

A cloud as big as the hand of a man.

JOSEPH.

Brews a storm in these mountains ?   'Tis bad !
God shield us this night !   Must I see
The Mother and Babe in the water-sheets drenched ?

MARY.

We will to the caves of the mountains creep.

JOSEPH.

And the leopards are there, the serpent and bear.

MARY.

And God !

JOSEPH.

God shield us this night !

Mary.

Joseph, trust!

Joseph.

The beast and the bird have caught the alarm;
The sun reddens low the cheek of the sky;
Night cometh with strides, and a night with storms.

NIGHT.

A citadel of rock there was, hoary
With years of crime, where centuries had gone
And robbers housed, nor man, to beard, had dared,
The bandit of the mountain in his den.

Joseph.

" His thunders, the heavens, journey round!"
" Deliver, good Lord!" within 'tis the thieves,
Without 'tis the tempest and night!

Mary.

We perish here! The Child! God drives us in!

The travellers knocking at the gate of the tower.)

And lo! the chieftain of that bold, bad band,
Touched by the trust, or by the heaven they bring,
Gives hospitality as Orient prince.

WITHOUT.

" His lightnings give shine, the world, unto ! "
" God thundereth marvellously ! "　" The pillars
Of heaven tremble ! "　" Thou, away, washest
The things that out of the earth grow ! "　" With God
Is majesty terrible ! "

WITHIN.

Spread is the couch, purple cloaks from the spoil,
Furs from the chase ; spread is the feast, the lamb
On th' spicy herbs of the mountains fattened,
Is broiled and garnished with olives and bread,
And wine from th' vines of Engaddi to warm
And to cheer ; spoils from the land, spoils from th' sea,
All are the robbers', sparing none, richest
And best, vultures of prey, where they may find.
Young Mary-mother, sweet tending her Babe,
Looking timidly on, fear in her heart,
Yet trust in the Father above.　A trust
For His Babe in her lap.　In her heart trust
And fear.　The robbers, fierce, swarthy, and dark,
Watching, curiously watching the mother
Tending so sweetly the Babe on her knee ;
And Joseph by, white and still in his dread.
And there was yet another, caring came,

Bearing in sweet dews from the mountain spring;
Resting on her knees, upholding the bowl,
As Mary, a-tremble, bathed th' beautiful Babe.
Was it the reverence in the mother's face
She saw, or the Babe on His mother's knees?
Beautiful Child! Saw she glow mid the curls,
Love in the eye, or the pity so young
On th' sweet Babe-lips; for she was a mother—
Oh, grief! her own dear boy a leper-child!
The wife of the chieftain, traditions[3] tell.
O, woman knelt there 'n beauty and paleness,
Once th' flower of the vale, the pride of a home,
Where the vines first flower when summer hath come,
Was it a curse for love unto sin?—Crash!
The thunders are at work in th' gorge below;
It was a night very like this her child
Was born; terrible night! terrible night!
That morning after—mornings alway come,—
A new joy lay asleep on her breast. ' Joy?'
Features her own, eyes of *his* when they looked
On her only, absolutely, tenderly.
But one spot, the smallest, over the heart.
Nought! nought! said the leech-crone of the mountains,
Haggard and old, bringing herbs for th' healing,
Ointments and washes and the lunar spells.
But yet this spot grew, she knew it would so;

Her heart took the penance at first glance in;
Grew over the rosy breast of the babe,
Slowly, but surely; daily a little
Over th' shoulders so dimpled and lovely,
Over the chest and each fair little limb,
Crept the slow white spot, leprously over;
There was no balm in Gilead, no leech there.
Shut out from all love but his, and this th' price,
Is it a wonder, and she a woman,
Her cheek, and her heart grew, with the spot,
One paler, one warmer?   Thus on her knees,
Looking wistfully on, in her heart is
Th' faith being born? The heart of the mother,
Doth it divine?   Rising up with the bowl
When the Christ-Child is washed, bearing the bowl
Up to her own little chamber remote,
Close to the couch where sleeps in his whiteness
Her own little boy as pale as the dead;
Fresh from such beauty her heart faints at th' sight.
A fragrance arises from the bowl.   Doth
She know what she doth?   She drops but a drop
On the white lips there; but a drop.   Her heart
Beats not, waiting t' know; but a drop. Sweet Christ?
Do they redden?   She sponges with her hand,
Every touch a prayer; holds to the taper
The hand from the water that had but washed

The Christ-Babe's hand.   Blessed water!   A glow!
Is it in th' flesh, or the flare of the lamp?
Can she wait—wait till the morning, to know?
O, never night on those mountains so long!
Nay, never night on those mountains so sweet!
God sendeth His calm, and the storms go down:
God sendeth His sleep, the eyes are a-close.
O, never night mid those mountains so sweet!
O, never morn on those mountains so bright!
Such blessing of healing, sweet Mary had borne
In her arms: Jesus and Mary had been
Taken in, the Child! th' Christ and His mother!
And the child who had lain down a leper,
All rosy and stainless and fair, the glow
Of the morning falls over the beautiful boy.

' Go!' said the robber and chief, ' go!' (perchance
He of his leprous boy thought when he took
Them in, when he saw a mother and child
In the storm, O, angels sweet! unawares);
' My roof it is blessed, yet unworthy its guests.
Take the path to the right of the cliff, that path—
And that; go!   Should a tribe's-man or any
These mountains that walk, stand dark in your path,
Say the name of the child that is healed!   Should
Ye lack for water, or bread, say the name

Of the child.   I need not bless ye ; ye are
Gods, and have blessed me ! '

                         The mother ?   Her eyes
A-beam through the tears, silence worships most—
Her lips melt on the guest-Babe's feet, wordless
For joy.
                   Laden with wine and bread they go,
Our three, down into the gorge where the tongue
Of the lightning had lapped the firs; up th' way
Where th' bolt of the cloud had riven the oak,
While the flower unscathed still bloomed at its roots,
The smile of the All-Beautiful coming
Afresh down over rock, ruin, and tree.
O, mountains of cedar ! vales after rains !
Long branches trailing brightness ! drenched flowers !
The glory of a morning after storms !
But the jewel of the legend remains
To be told—saith the tradition, this child
That was healed, thirty-three years and after,
Was the penitent thief of the cross.

CHAPTER III.

IN THE DESERT.

PART I.

Scene—*Silhor, the land of the Amalekite, entering the Desert.*

SILHOR'S rock-bedded stream is forded now,
Two days are measured on the sunny banks
Where brilliant flowers with tropic luxuriance feast
The gentle eye, the beautiful, that loves.
The border of that enemy of old, where God
For Israel fought, and Moses' wearied arms
Were stayed, is passed.   The desert opens next,
Flowerless; ay, blossomless as stolid souls
Who love not God's flower-leafings, or His birds,
Those things that seem most for their beauty made,
And in poor scorn of a Creator's works,
Forget how He must love to form, and think
Them good, or wherefore made such plenitude?
The barren desert frowning opens next,
Way dreaded, in the wake of caravan,
With faithful guide and hardy camel-train;
Yet they shrink not.
       Learn, ye despairing ones,
Who sickened oft by life's rough wayside faint,

When ye this bleak world find a desert drear,
Learn of these holy travellers to count
Not dangers in the way that God has marked.

PART II.

LOST IN THE DESERT.

In unknown deserts plunged, the hot winds rise;
No point they seek lies in the shifting sand,
And there are days the sullen sun is hid,
And nights the guiding moon and stars come not,
Till Joseph, foot-sore grown and weak, would fain
Have pillowed in the desert solitude
His fainting head, and welcomed earth's last rest.

JOSEPH (*sinking down.*)

The red wind of the desert is out to night,
Perish we must, O, Mary, my maid!

But Mary in her arms the Christ-Child bears,

And looking up in prayer,
She sees a light afar,
And knows it is an angel's eye,
'Tis brighter than a star,

And fainteth not, sweet spouse, but soothingly
And well speaketh the kind encouragement
That woman's lips best whisper to the heart
Of man when bordering on a void despair.
The pain is in her heart, that boding pain
Left of the sword that Simeon saw, yet now
The Babe is on her breast that charms all pain.

PART III.

MIRACLE OF THE DESERT.

Nine days [4] in the desert lost,
On a sea of sand-waves tost,
    Quaffed the last sweet drink of water,
Down our pilgrims sink and sigh ;
Down, perchance, to sleep and die ;
Nay, in weakness He is nigh,
    He who shields fair Sion's daughter.

Lo ! His angel-bands appear,
And the fainting sleepers near,
    And the nearest angel sings
As he scatters from his hands
Golden seed upon the sands,
With his wing the plantage fans
    Till the quickened seed up-springs.

Straight another's shining shaft
Cleaves the ground unto its haft,
    Following which the waters rush
With a low and murmuring sound,
Eddying in a circle round,
Form a basin in the ground,
    Where a-brim the cool waves gush.

One plants germs of purple fruit,
Whence the sappy vines they shoot;
    Another makes the bread-tree rise,
Doth the fountain-border sow,
Makes the fruited fig-tree grow,
And the fragrant orange blow:
    And still the golden seed it flies.

Boungavilla's purple bloom
Gives the visioned night perfume,
    Poinsetta's azure streamers
Floating from the cocoa trees,
Waving in the wooing breeze,
And the bamboo's widening leaves
    Hedge around the peaceful dreamers.

Grasses creep o'er Mary's bed,
Lilies flower about her head,
    Daffodils below her feet,

And a stately sandal fair
Spreads its odorous branches there,
Casts its perfume in her hair,—
  Babe and mother slumbering sweet.

Yet, afar, another plants,
And the beauteous palm up-slants,
  Straight its trunk forms tall and fair,
'Neath the breath the angel breathes
Growing branches clothe with leaves;
Round uprise the sweet spice-trees,
  Clove and cassia scent the air.

There is the banana's store
Tinted golden to the core,
  Sprinkled 'tween with varied flower,
There the scented menepsa grows,
Here the ripened mango glows,
Buds the crimson-burning rose;
  Angels planting till the matin-hour.

Hides each tree, a birdling's nest;
Painted butterfly at rest,
  Every tiny flower-cup folds:
At morn each happy bird will sing,
Each insect try its gilded wing,
From grassy tuft a buzz will ring,
  That now the beetle holds.

As morning o'er the desert breaks,
Mary first in wonder wakes—
  'God is gracious unto me!
How this herbage green could grow,
How that blessed fountain flow,
Only God and angels know!
  Joseph! Joseph! wake and see!

'Slept we not in desert-land
Mid a sea of scorching sand?
  I have heard it said, in death,
The sweet, refreshing spring appears,
The lay of singing birds one hears,
With blossoms bright the palm-tree nears
  And scents the failing breath.

'Is this desert-death?   Ah, no!
This Child could not perish so;
  Sweetest proof that God is love.
Let us tarry yet a day,
In this oasis rest and pray,
Ere we seek refreshed our way:
  We are in the care above.'

CHAPTER IV.

BY THE NILE.

AT the hidden head of Nilus,
   Veiled a thousand years or more,
Lo, I stand lost in gloaming
   Down the old historic shore.

This is Egypt and her river!
   'What is Egypt? What to me?
There's a Flower from Palestine,
   Only which I yearn to see!'

But the skies are bright above thee,
   With an Egypt-depth of blue,
And the pyramids of old
   Limn the distant desert-view.

There's the house Sesostris built,
   Stones to keep his name forever;
Stones are silent, lost his doorway,
   Onward flows the lasting river.

Aged Egypt! Glorious river!
   'What is Egypt? What to me?

7

There's a Flower from Palestine,
  Only which I yearn to see ! '

Cities rise, Memphis, On, and Thebes,
  Egypt's idols, art, and pride ;
Purple sails and golden barges
  Float adown the worshipped tide.

Here, raining down o'er templed roofs,
  Dropped the matin of old Memnon
Daily as the morning travailed
  With the birth of her great sun.

There, the old Pharonic splendors
  Dazed as destinies unrolled,
And the Cleopatrian grandeurs
  Stirred the passion of a world.

' Lo, I heed not, not the wile,
  Not the spell and necromancies,
Hieroglyphics, mummies, lore,
  Palace, temple, mysteries,

' All are paling on my vision;
  What is Egypt ?   What to me ?
There's a Flower from Palestine,
  Only which I yearn to see !

' I have tracked the desert-wild,
Following one vision mild—
Where is Mary and the Child ? '

In the glorious Nilus wood,
Near the heart of solitude,
In the gem of lotus-bowers
'Mid a paradise of flowers.

' Lotus-bloomings ! Queenly ? ' No ;
All too dainty leafed in snow.
' Fair ? ' Ay, voluptuous, in sense
Of full flower and redolence
Of sweets and beauteousness ;
But the rare voluptuousness
Of each creamy petal white,
Streaked with crimson softly bright,
Breathing but of Paradise ;
White, glow-tinged flakes of incense,
' Goddess-flowers,' scent the air,
Fan her blessed forehead fair,
Sweetly recollected sank
On thy richly verdant bank.
Turned to jewels in the wave,
Where the arrowy noonbeams lave,

Sporting in the sunlight glance,
Where the gem-winged insects dance,
Up where trees majestic nod
To the flower-enamelled sod,
With its gorgeous petals spread,
Lifting high a queenly head,
Where the Egypt-lily blows,
Where the blue flag taller grows,
Where the swan with beauty grave
Spreads his white wing o'er the wave,
Beam those tranquil eyes o'er all;
Over all, yet ever constant fall
With a recollected wonder,
And a world more tender ponder,
On the young Child at her feet,
Of more than babe beauty sweet,
With the rose-acacia round
His fair temples lightly bound ;
Precious Jesus ! roses now !
Must a thorn-wreath bind that brow ?
But I leave the after woe,
To the hour God will show !
Recollected maid of grace,
Suffer us thy thought to trace.

Mary.

Waved in gold, old, generous river,
Light and shade around thee quiver ;
On thy bank's enchanting water
Glows the heart of Jacob's daughter.
Thou hast memories for the Jew,
Once another mother drew
Sorrowing to thy solemn tide
With the babe she could not hide ;
In an ark of rushes wrought,
All her heart that mother brought ;
A thousand years ere-since have flown,
And yet I list her stifled moan,
And even now in yonder shade
I see her bend above her babe,
Shut up the ark with trembling hands,
And anguished slide it from the sands :
I see the nearing maiden-train
That winds across the flowery plain ;
I know in Nilus' worshipped wave
A royal princess comes to bathe ;
Th' captured boat, th' lifted lid, and lo, appears
The babe all beautiful in tears !
Now in artless infant wile
Looking up with sweet babe-smile.

Babe, to Egypt we have fled,
Love, to shield thy princely head;
And the thought abides with me,
Child, that he was type of Thee;
He withstood the power of pride,
Egypt's favor cast aside,
And when Israel was distressed,
Chose his lot with the oppressed;
(Thou must thus, my Sacred Son,
Earthly pomp and purples shun;)
Forty years by desert-fountain
Fed his flock on Horeb-mountain,
Till by high command he came
Israel's freedom to proclaim;
Through the parted Red-Sea bed
Jacob's hosts in triumph led;
Ah! the great lawgiver died
On the Jordan's desert-side.
Died?   Tradition runs he laid
Asleep in Nebo's sacred shade,
Whom the High God stooped to kiss,[5]
And he fainted with the bliss,
Ecstasied in sweet surprise,
Awoke in Paradise.
Will my darling Jesus die?
Why, my Dove, that boding sigh?

Moses was but born of earth;
Thine is a celestial birth.

Ah! the sword in vision now
Brings the shadow to her brow;
All the blood her cheek forsook,
Down the prophets runs a startled look;
And she bends with tearful gaze
Till those pleading hands upraise
Caught unto her loving bosom,
Glows He there her sacred blossom;
Tender Ruby above price!
Beauteous Babe of Paradise!
All her soul in mirror lies
In the heaven of His eyes;
And those Christ-sweet lips to kiss
Is the Virgin Mother's bliss.

  Soft she kisses,
And her heart is love-encalmed;
  And caresses,
And her very hand is balmed.

Blessed mother! adoring the Child, fondling the Child! Glorious Child! Tenderly glorious Child!

MARY.

From mine this human heart first warmed
  And drew its crimson flood;

Yet still my inmost soul bows down
And worships Thee as God.

As God! No earthly child e'er wore
Such cherub-beauty fair;
So bright on every clustering curl,
The glory haloed there.

Thou art my Rose of Sharon, Boy,
Thy bloom caught from above,
And I will wear my Angel-Flower
With meekest mother-love.

Yet never need fear love too well,
So closely linked with mine
The sacred, dear humanity,
Incarnate Bud Divine!

O Son, so marvellously mine,
O son, and yet my God,
I give my heart, my life, my love,
My worship as my blood!

CHAPTER V.

EGYPTIAN PEASANTS.

Egyptian.

RETURNING from the city mart this morn,
Sawest thou, Charmion, where the palms thicken
At th' first bend of th' Nile, a Hebrew tent [6]
Pitched cozily ?   But late from Syria I wot.

Charmion.

Ay, at the tent-door stood, my lord.

Egyptian.

Hey ! lookèd in !   Well, it was woman-like,
And well enough this once, in sooth.   What saw ?

Charmion.

What might feast royal eyes, of womanhood
The Rose, upon a couch of moss fresh spread,
Her breast upon, the Pearl of Beauty, bright
As if but just from the pure heavens out-dropped.

Egyptian.

Ay, Beauty and her Babe !   Didst greet them kind,
My Charmion, the gentle strangers' due ?

7*

Charmion.

Nay, slumber like of silver mist a veil,
Lay soft each breathing lip upon, sweet twain!
Thus shut me off, yet left the joy to look.
O, it was pleasure to the eyes, the fair
And delicately moulded arm by sleep
Relaxed still o'er the bright babe spread like wing
Of mother-dove over the brooded nest.
Wordless I gazed, as fast my soul grew warm,
In silent worship bowed, I kissed the hem
Of their scant robes; a bottle of sweet wine
And basket of ripe olives left I laid
For my peace-offering at their beauteous feet,
And turned with a hushed step away, saying
Unto myself the while, That fair young creature,
When she wakes, will wondering see, and ask,
Have the gods sent a love-gift while I slept
Unto my babe and me?

Egyptian.

           Ours is a land
Of bread and pleasant fruits and golden gains,
And holds of lore the key. Perchance they come
To drink of the sweet Nile, and daily bathe
In our luxurious air, forgetting toil,
And sterner climes, to know the joy it is

To live nigh to the rich, warm heart of earth ;
Or yet they may have crossed a tyrant's wrath.

Charmion.

Aught else than ill.   I saw them when the soul
Is outside worn, and limns on lip and brow.

Egyptian.

I would not doubt the verdict of thy eyes ;
And thou art pleasured, tender Charmion,
I take it best.

Charmion.

   To-morrow I will pluck
And carry them the ripest melon found
Upon our vines.

   The kindness-bread, the waves
Upon ye cast, peasants of Egypt-land,
Increased a hundred fold, the Great Unknown
Shall give it back ; His Christ none serve,
His Christ, or His, nor win the blessing back.

CHAPTER VI.

THE FIRST WORD.

THE flower that veers to watch the journeying sun,
　　That nodded gayly to the Orient
At morn, bowed westwardly its yellow crown,
And all the flowering tribes aggrieved drew close
Their petal robes each perfumed heart about.
The sun had gone, gone with his givings down ;
Earth, as some rich-souled woman when her lover
Has but gone, stands in the glow of dear farewells,
En-rainbowed with the past, looking both night
And morning in the face. Earth, fair earth, stood,
And Twilight in her pensive beauty leaned
On the horizon-threshold (as some saint
To list the evening hymn of Nature sweet,
Ascending from the wilderness, or cot,
Of mellow bird, or human voice of prayer,
God's good works goodly praising Him, for day,
For night), as slow the regal night drew on,
One hand with silver gloved laid soft a-down
His broad and dusky-handed palm within—
Absorbed, nocturnal purples deepened round,
A poet looked up and sang, ' Day kisses

Night.   The sky is all a-blush !   The Future
And the Past join hands.   His sun He maketh
Journey down, darkness to cover earth.   Good
Is the Lord, and good His works.'

Sweet Mary,

Lo, at her rustic door, clasping her child,
Looks out upon the purpling west and sees
Him in the sunset cloud.   One little hand
Uplifts unto her lips with touch that swift
Recalls those love-o'erbrimming eyes.   O, child !
Creator-Child by whom the very world
Was made !   That dimpled hand is kissed.
O, for a kiss upon our brow in death
Like that ! to draw us straight to Heaven ! Hush ! soft !
Upon her Christ-Babe gazes she !   Gazes,
Asking her heart the sweet maternal name
Will this Divine Child ever give ?
To me, an earthly woman ! Lord ?   Caressingly
Her neck about a rosy arm entwines,
And quick as warble soft of birdling's note,
And musically clear as cherub-tone,
In answer to her humble thought, out-drops
Th' first sweet word, and that sweet word is ' *mother.* '[8]

CHAPTER VII.

THE RETURN.

PART I.

RECALL.

FOR THEY ARE DEAD.—MATT. ii.

THE sceptred hand unclasps and palsied falls,
A crownèd head in deathly terror bows;
He who woke stricken Rachel's piercing wail,
His arrow feels who on the pale horse rides;
Where Mariamne's pallid ghost awaits,
And murdered sons, and Bethlehem's bleeding babes,
To reckon not up war-feud's blood-red fields,
Or Day that pends, gone down into the shades:
And the e'er-mindful Lord forgetteth not
His Son Beloved; by Joseph's tranquil couch
The white-robed angel stands that twice before
Hath on his midnight slumbers softly broke:
That same bright brow hath a familiar look,
That voice celestial a remembered tone,
And Joseph in his sleep looks trusting up,
Rejoicing in the Heaven-permit, 'Seek ye
Your father-land,' "for they are dead."

PART II.

DEPARTURE.

Lovelier than erst
On Nilus banks the golden morning breaks;
As setting suns the most attractive glow,
As gathered roses sweetest odors shed,
As our winged "blessings brighten in their flight,"
Lovelier than erst.
Ye shady banks that have
In sojourn grown fast wondrous dear, so soon
The yearning heart roots unto what is beautiful
And near.   Ye trees that at the evening wore
But distant look, or nodded passing cool,
Like old friends round the tender farewell claim,
And every palmy nook where Mary 's knelt
To pray, must have its lingering adieu.
There is the bower where she hath told her Boy,
To her Christ-Boy, traditions of the fatherland,
Of Judah and her prophets stoned, until
He wept.   There is a tree, th' sweet mimosa,
Nearest the door, the Cottage of the Nile:
How oft beneath she and her child had sat;
There was the place the young Child learned to walk;
That morn the tree was in its brightest flower,

But soon as e'er His feet the green turf pressed,
Its glorious boughs stirred like a harp,
And straight the yellow flowers of fragrance dropped
Like stars of gold upon the favored turf.
That tree that cast its bright crown at His feet,
And with bared boughs rejoiced with her, that tree
Looks down upon her now.   Was it a wind
The branches swept, or does it sigh?   With tears
One sweet memorial-spray is plucked.   Dear tree!
But Joseph hurries on.   The caravan,
The yearly caravan is on its move.
To Egypt's pleasant groves and the bright Nile
One lingering glance is fondly cast.   Farewell!
'Farewell, O gorgeous plains of Egypt-land!
One sod of Palestine is worth ye all!'

PART III.

CANAAN.

Ho, border-land!   The Canaan lies before!
Mount Carmel's purple top, contrasting rich
With the soft yellow sky in which it looms,
Arises with a grandeur more than erst.
Ho, Judah's blue hill-tops!   Mountains of God,
All-hail!

Upon the first home-sod, Mary
Her young son rests, and sinks in adoration
At His feet.   Joseph, pure patriarch, lost
In gladness on the green earth falls to praise.

PART IV.

(Joseph having just heard that Archelaus is king.)

O, dear is Joseph's town, but dearer far
That sacred mother and that sacred Child ;
Toward fair but lovely Nazareth he turns,
As prophet of the Lord long since hath wrote ;
As oft may we from free act careful choose,
And yet but an accordant move with Heaven.
Meekly in silent waiting, though with heart
That yearned toward Nazareth, meek Mary sat
The saddled mule upon, till Joseph turned
Unto the path the old mule recognized,
And trod on with a fresher step toward home.

PART V.

HOME.

O, home, returned to after absent years,
Greeted with heart-swells never felt before ;
And yet, the hills are higher than of old,
The ancient village-site strangely outgrown

A fair daguerreotype worn in the heart :
The graves are thicker sewn within the place
Of tombs, and on the old dear ones, the weeds
Are rank and tall; and brows of friends have change,
Or wrinkles gathered on; the blithesome maids
Late left, are wives with young babes lisping now
Around their knees; and prattling children then,
Are goodly youths quite grown and damsels tall.
Ah, there is sadness in the longed-for hour
That puzzles sore the memory-haunted heart.
Seven [9] lost years broaden well a chasm deep
For loving heart to come up instant to ;
Mary, gentlest of women, feels the gulf,
But looks into her God-Boy's eyes, and stays
Her tears.   There is her grief, and there her joy !
" O Trinity of earth ! "   O Holy Family !
Poor Nazareth is rich in ye, erewhile
From her despised streets one Nazarene
Shall come whose brows a ransomed world shall crown !

NOTES TO BOOK IV.

1. A TRADITION, I do not recollect by whom transmitted, says: One day the Virgin, in their flight, sat down hungry and weary under a barren date tree, when it suddenly fruited, and Joseph and she joyfully partook of the dates.

> 2. First to die for Christ, sweet lambs,
> At the very altars ye
> Sport in your simplicity.—PRUDENTIUS.

Thus Prudentius; but we had only read the touching Testament record, and were not even aware that these Holy Innocents had long been classed among the martyrs by the Latin and Greek churches, till some years after this scene was first written, it being among one of the earliest chapters.

3. The holy family in their flight passed a night in a robber's cave, or citadel, as some have it. The wife of the chieftain had a young leper son, whom she washed in the water where the Virgin had bathed the young Child, and her son was healed from that hour; and this boy, afterward a robber, was the penitent thief of the cross.

4. For the germ and groundwork of this scene we are indebted to Abbé Gerbet: see his *Lily of Israel;* though we have followed the pious allegory, as he relates it, but in part.

5. "The Jews have a tradition that Moses died of the kisses of God's lips."

6. Cairo, Alexandria, Hermopolis, and Heliopolis, all have been assigned as the place of their residence while in Egypt. Baronius tells us that near the gate of Heliopolis grew a large peach tree, beneath which Satan had been worshipped. As they entered the gate, Satan took his flight, and the tree bowed to the ground as they passed, and the fruit, leaves, and bark afterward had the power of healing. Alexandria has the support of the fact that it had been colonized by Jews in 330, 322, and 312 B. C., and had a large and flourishing synagogue.

7. "Cornelius a Lapide (Lib. I.) says that many Egyptians, touched by the sanctity of these blessed spouses, adored and loved the true God."

8. When Mary would have taught Him the sweet name, mother, her soul was troubled. Was such glory for her reserved, her, but a feeble woman? With humility she remained silent; but whether the Holy Child had brought it from heaven, or learned it from some woman of the hamlet teaching her infant, He pronounced it one day like a bird beginning to warble under the mother-bird's wing.—*Vide Abbé Gerbet.*

9. Here the Fathers of traditionary history differ. One says nine, others five, three, and two years the holy family remained in Egypt. Ammonius of Alexandria, whose opinion we have favored, has it seven years. Epiphamus thought our Lord was two years old when He fled, and remained in Egypt two. Maldonatus fixes it at not less than four and not more than seven years. Baronius argues that He fled in His first year, and returned in His ninth; which opinion Suarez also favors

BOOK V.

OR

BOOK OF MIRACLES.

Then came the three years' ministry; and it seemed as if the Babe of Bethlehem, or the Boy of Nazareth, had been nothing to the Preacher of love, whose words and works of miracles appeared to charge the world with more of supernatural beauty than it could bear.—Faber.

CONTENTS.

CHAPTER I.

> " In sunny vales of Palestine,
>   By sparkling fount and rill,
> And by the sacred Jordan's stream,
>   And o'er each vine-clad hill,
> Once lived and roved the fairest Child
>   That ever blessed the earth ;
> The happiest, the holiest
>   That e'er had human birth."

BEHOLD HE STANDETH SHEWING HIMSELF THROUGH THE LATTICE.—CANTICLES.

" JESUS CHRIST a boy ! " The thought startles back and dis-
tances reach. The sprightliness, the exuberance of boyhood, ever
and anon the Deity brightening through the humanity, outshining
in spontaneous acts of little kindnesses. The eye of the soul drifts
back to the Babe of the manger, surveys the Man of Sorrows and of
Calvary. But where standeth the Christ-Boy limned ? The Divine
nature hidden under the speechless, passive human, the God taber-
nacled in its silent sanctuary, is a felt mystery. Yet babehood in
its waiting hush, negative greatness, wistful uncertainty, possible
undeveloped majesty of manhood, is itself a mystery, and somehow
better holds the thought of a divinity, a silent, hidden God. As
still flowers upon which we look, and they vanish not, arises the
clear, beautiful vision of the Immanuel Babe and Bethlehem ; but
the Immanuel Boy, the gleams of His spiritual beauty, the celestial
gracefulness of His every light motion flash in upon our indistinct
vision as the brilliant wings of the paradise birds upon the dreams
of the olden poets. There, brilliantly there, and away ! melted in

8

rapt air, as the rainbow in the blue, lost in the spiritual, and God a Boy is still an impalpable mystery; and the Nazareth where He dwelt, well nigh as remotely shut from out our Christendom as the Eden garden and its originally glorious pair. As the Eden? More! Hath not a Milton sung of the Eden and its Eve, but an English-tongued bard of the Nazareth and its Mary—where? Forgive us, Christ of Nazareth, and take us in! With the feebleness of the earth trembles our song, with the breaks of a harp unskilled; yet our heart groweth reverent more, gazing afar. Take us in! "My be-loved, behold he standeth shewing himself through the lattice"—at the lattice,

> Where the palm and where the flower
> Half the holy house embower;

where the rose-laurels brighter bloom; where the spikenard giveth forth sweeter scent than elsewhere in all sweet-scented Palestine. "Open unto me, O my beloved!" Open thy gates, O paradise of innocence! Walls that shelter and surround an indwelling God, we salute thee! Home-temple of the Christ, we salute thee! con-secrate are thy door-posts, beams, floor-way, and thatch! Home of the Virgin Mother and her God-born, Easternly and quaintly, lovely as lowly, screened half by fruited palm and climbing rose; the equatorial glory falleth brightly as the years lapse on; within, the Sidonian loom has its niche; the red cedar distaff hangs on the wall, and the spinning-wheel of Anna the sainted stands by the lat-tice, the lily-pot beside with its one lily in flower, as in the day when Anna spun, and looked through the casement and beheld the beautiful maiden of Nazareth under the trees of the garden, to whom Gabriel came down at the twilight as she was at prayer.

O Nazareth-daughter and mother returned from the Egypt-land and the Nile-valley, come back to the olden and sacred and dear, to the hamlet and garden and cot, from the flight and the desert and the exile back! O, pattern for all the daughters of the Lord! O, for one glimpse in and upon the beautiful life! where

Meekly in her moss-thatched cot,
"Brown as a last-year bird-nest,"
Sweet content withal and blest,
Mary takes her lowly lot;
Round the radiant years are rolled,
As a wheel each spoke of gold.

All the graces of a wife
And a mother clustered round,
Time for all the duties found,
Time for hours of holy life,
As the fruitful years are told,
Gathered days as sheaves of gold.

Not a sorrow brings alloy,
Heavenliest days that upward fly,
Years that all glide mystic by
With but brilliancy of joy;
Brightest life to mortal given
This side of the gate of heaven.

Blessed Nazareth Mother! "All the glory of the king's daughter is in the interior of her house"—the Christ. What a source of happiness to spin and weave his linen tunic, and embroider his holiday vesture; "and how she hung on His looks, His words, His gestures!" Simeon hath spoken, and the memory abides in her heart. "The stormy sea of the judicial world on which so many and such illustrious prophets had been wrecked, lies beneath her clear vision;" but her Son is with her now. "The storm still howls in the distance," and the wise Virgin of the Scripture heedeth not to take the dark morrow in, shutting out the young Christ and bright to-day. And He, the richly silent Child, the calm, mysterious Boy, whose outward life, while yet so beautifully still, " was light and fragrance all," dwelt with her in the Nazareth cottage days and months and years, and over her of the fragrance of His own fragrant life cast, she in the overshadowed bloom of Deity, growing beautiful alway, He who " had a Father in the heavens whom the seraphim proclaimed thrice-holy," having a mother on the earth scented by the fragrance of all virtues, " wanting not the splendors of holiness," purest, raptest, human holiness. O, fairest earth-saint, living with Jesus all the day long, all the years long! O, lovingest saint-mother, rearing the Christ!

> Sweetest life to mortal given
> This side of the gate of heaven!

Living with Jesus *and His Mother!* Mother of Jesus! could we give thee a sweeter name? Held the earth ever name so sweet? *One—Jesus.* AVE MATER JESU!

> Sweet the beauty of the hidden Rose
> Soft through all the ages glows,
> At whose lattice Christians joy
> Still to gaze on Christ a Boy.

CHAPTER II.

LOST.

PART I.

SCENE—*Feast of Tabernacles at Jerusalem; hour of worship in the temple.*

WEEK of a nation's penitence and prayer!
    For suppliants, Jerusalem is full!
I see but three: Joseph the just,
The man, the representative who stands
And shadows the Eternal Father there;
I see him in the temple kneel, and she,
Sweet Mother of our Lord, the Christ between.
I see but three, and hearken Mary's hymn
More sweet than all the spices offered there:
And lo, He with the name unspeakable,
The Everlasting Lord, just twelve years old,
The Incarnate prayeth on the earth!
Do songs go on in heaven, or angels fold
All timorously hushed their happy wings,
Mute worshippers, as looms the prayer
Of a co-equal God, the throne before? [1]

PART II.

ACCORDING TO THE CUSTOM OF THE JEWS.—LUKE ii.

SCENE—*A caravan returning from the feast; Cleophas, Salome, Mary, and others.*

SALOME.

It is a solemn feast, our Passover.

CLEOPHAS.

The pasch our fathers ate, the staff in hand,
As past the lintel-post, blood-stained, the stern
And swift destroying angel flashed to smite
Proud Egypt's firstborn, from the princely heir
Of Pharaoh's throne to dungeoned captive's son :
The memory of an hour like that it's well
With solemn pomp to mark.

SALOME.

It should be thus.

CLEOPHAS.

And yet it late-time seemeth unto me,
It is not kept as in the days when I
Was but a child.

SALOME.

Thus unto me ; yet still,
'Tis good to go up to these feasts ; each time
Our heart seems sensibly enlarged toward Him,
Whose mercies, fresh as Hermon's dews, fail not.

CLEOPHAS.

Ay, goodly is the sight when Simeon
From village southernmost sends up his sons,
And Reuben from beyond Abarim Mount,
Naphtali where the Lebanons look down,
Manassas from the Jordan's other side,
Or Aser from his olive-spotted shore
By the mild inlets of the western sea ;
When Jacob's tribes from every vine-clad hill,
From every city of the plain appear,
Brethren of Israel's one family—

SALOME.

For prayer ; and thus their hearts grow knit and they—

CLEOPHAS.

Who travel thus, are strangers never more.

MARY.

I miss my Son !

Salome.

And are not mine with Him,
My sons ? When the tents pitch, straightway we'll search
Them out.　Joseph will give good heed.　Fear not !

PART III.

"They halted where a cedar hung
Its shadow o'er a sparkling rill,
And spread their meal of simple fare."

O, goodly is the sight of Israel
In booths, of waving palm, of supper spread,
And they who gather there, old patriarchs
In the ripe glory of their blossomed locks,
And young men in their strength of years, matrons
Of pleasant gravity, and maidens chaste
As beautiful, and littler damsels eyed
Like antelopes ; fair boys—but Mary's son,
The pearl of all ?　Not there !　Nor hath he yet
With Joseph been.　Apart the mother stands,
Confounded in her grief, and would have turned
Into the darkness back ; but broken was
The way and rough, the tiger-jungle near ;
' Within Jerusalem safe housed, the Boy
Was doubtless well ; ' and she was stayed, waiting
The morn ; yet biding not the voice of hope

And comforting, alone she stands, and they
Whose words of pity fail fall reverent back,
As out beneath the pitying stars she weeps,
Or keeps the narrow circle of her tent
And feels the loneliness, the utter night,
The barren void all of her children feel
When Christ goes sudden out the heart where He
Hath late in burning brightness tender dwelt;
As the Forlorn One yet shall hang and cry,
" Why hast thou me forsook? " Yet, wherefore strive
To word the dolor sharp ? We only know
That all is deeps of anguish and of night;
The human smote, amazed, the God withdrawn.

Apart she stands, confounded in her grief,
And questions as a mother and a saint: .
Could He have followed on and lost the track,
Or was he prey to wild beast by the way ?
Was this the sword that Simeon saw, and had
It come so soon ? Or yet, unworthy had
She proved ; and had the Father taken back
The gift, His Son ? Ah, how could He have left,
Unsaid ? Her Christ-Boy kind ! Oh, never, He !
Her head had lain the desert-sands amid,
Yet happy with the Christ her arms within ;
And distant, doleful Calvary will bring

8*

The bitter blessedness to share with Him;
Yet wherefore strive to word the dolor dark?
We only know a child is lost, the bright
And beautiful Immanuel Boy! and she,
The mother of that boy, and he, the kind
And anxious foster-sire, seek sorrowing,
Seek by the way, seek at the city gates,
Seek through the streets of long Jerusalem,
And find Him not.   Oh, hope, dear hope deferred,
How sick it makes a heart!

Mary.

I cannot give
Him up! and yet I faint. Sweet Boy! Oh, Son!

Joseph.

We'll search until we die, sad spouse; 'twere sweet
To die a-searching and we find Him not.

Mary.

" Tell me, of Zion, Oh, ye daughters, tell,
My fair Beloved have ye seen? "

Women of Jerusalem.

" And what
More than another's is thy Beloved?
O, thou fairest among women! "

Mary.

‘ His head

As gold, His eyes are as of doves the eyes,
Rivers of waters by—the Jordan pure,
His cheeks as beds of spices fresh, as flowers,
His lips as lilies dropping fragrance sweet,
Yea, altogether lovely He, lovely
And first, chieftest among ten thousand fair.’

Women of Jerusalem.

First Group.

And such an one we saw, such angel-boy,
Some three days gone, leading poor Bartemas
The blind, safe through a rude and jostling crowd.

Second Group.

And we, such an one, scarce two days past,
Perhaps ’t was yesterday, pouring some oil
Into the sores of Lazarus, th’ beggar,
That lies with dogs without the city gates.

Third Group.

And we such child this morning straight beheld,
Go like a spirit up the temple way.

Forsaken mother, day beams on Zion’s towers !
Go in.

PART IV.

*Academic Hall of the Temple, Jesus in the midst of the doctors,
Mary and Joseph entering at the door.*

And she, His mother, standing at that door,
Suspended in her joy.   The angel brush
We lack, and would not daub.   Ye who have hearts,
Ye who've children, yet not a Jesus-boy,
Look in and see !

        I had this scene portrayed
Unto me once—a moment once, by one
Of bolder thought, and straight a view unrolled,
Would show you how old Jewish doctors looked,
All of the pentateuch, their brows beneath,
Amazed !   Lo, there, familiar with the scribe,
He stands, that meek Boy of twelve summers fair.
The sunbeams glance through golden window-bars,
And flash along the gem-lit walls to pour
Their gathered glory round.   His tunic-folds
Unto a silvery whiteness turned, the curls
Like drops of virgin gold on that child-brow,
Divinely fair, like some young priest descended
From star, or sun he stands and talks the law.
Now from His lips touched with lingering echo
Of the heavens such answers calmly roll,
Taking the keen spirit of the law up

So sweepingly, "old hard-faced Jews" standing
In the bold background out, Rabbi Aaron,
Long-bearded, looking so wise, Nicodemus,
Marvellous old questioner, sagacious,
Lion-eyed Gamaliel, interpreters
Of Moses, are staggered back! amazed!

Wonderful wisdom! Wonderful holiness! " She found in an
ineffable way the Beloved whom she sought."

PART V.

"AND HIS MOTHER SAID UNTO HIM, SON, WHY HAST THOU THUS DEALT
WITH US?"

> " We lost thee ere the stars did shine,
>   And lo, we sought thee sorrowing.
>
> .   .   .   .   .   .
>
>   His answer sank into her soul!
>   It seemed to paint His Passion's hour
>   In blood upon time's wondrous scroll:
>   'O, woman! knowest thou not,' He said,
>   'How lapse the hours, my years how few,
>   Or wouldst thou that thy love delayed
>   My Father's work, that I must do?'"

"AND THEY UNDERSTOOOD NOT THE SAYING UNTO THEM .   .   .   .   BUT
HIS MOTHER KEPT ALL THESE SAYINGS IN HER HEART."

SCENE—*Without the city gate, journeying to Nazareth.*

And Jesus closer to her drew, and she
Her Love unto her given back, Her Son
As from the dead, more dear forevermore!
She takes his hand and journeys on toward home.

PART VI.

AND JESUS INCREASED IN WISDOM AND STATURE, AND IN FAVOR WITH
GOD AND MAN.

While Joseph, worn by journeyings, years and toil,
Learned his wood-craft to the young Carpenter
And rested from his cares—

                        Behold, O world!
Take heart, poor laborer!   Look up!   A God
Hath taken homely labor in His hands,
And henceforth blessed all honest toil; and made
It as God's work, honorable!   Ye delve: Christ did.

CHAPTER III.

IN MEMORIAM.

THE PATH OF THE JUST AS A SHINING LIGHT GOETH FORTH AND IN-
CREASETH EVEN TO PERFECT DAY.—PROV.

Not until after death their blissful crown
Others obtain, but unto thee was given
In thine own lifetime to enjoy thy God
As do the blest in heaven .

Vesper Hymn, Feast of St. Joseph.

To dwell amidst God's mysteries of grace and to be familiarly conver-
sant with them, is as it were the renewal of that vesper walk with the living God which was the privilege of our first father, while yet unfallen and
standing upright among the glorious trees of Paradise in the celestial
beauty of his original justice.—FABER.

THE Eden life of Adam is renewed.   O, man most favored of
God! holding His highest honors and office on earth.   Representa-

tive father! Happy thou who didst believe! Happy thou who didst take the Child first from the arms of His mother! First man to hold God in his arms! Happy thou who didst share the desert and Egypt, and earn bread by the sweat of thy brow for the mother and Child—a garment for the young Messias! There are thirty-three years that are jewels in the cycles of time. Thirty of these years fell to the years in the life of Joseph. Sharing nigh the full length of the " Hidden Life," the presence immediate, intimate of " the God with us," Jesus-Immanuel, and then taken home ere the golden cord of those years is loosed, ere the axe is laid at the foot of the beautiful tree, the beautiful Saviour-tree of a world! Ere the scourge and the cross break his loving old heart. Whoever but him came so near? Whoever but him lived so long with the Christ, and the cup passed his lips? O, the goodness of God unto Joseph! Joseph, name laden with benedictions and repose. The old patriarch has leaned down on his staff more and more of late; a pilgrim crossing slowly serene the border-land, walking through Beulah, beautiful Beulah! leisurely, tranquilly, his heart and his prayers gone on before; his just works gone on before! Dear old man! mildly glorious old saint, bearing quietly on.

Vesper purples the vales below; a crown of halos, or the sunset loth to leave hangs over the cot; the Rose of Jericho leans her red cheek more tenderly close to the lattice; the jessamines swaying at the casement, from their golden cups shedding perfume to the airs without, and incensing chamber and couch within, where the sire of the cot, " a shock fully ripe," the patriarch and pilgrim, has laid aside sandals and staff.

L IST! There is a slow but certain
Rustle of the white couch-curtain!
Hear I not a mystic tapping
At our hallowed cottage-door?
Hear I not the Death-King rapping?
Angel-footsteps on the floor?

Agèd Joseph heareth faintly,
And he smileth, O, how saintly

Mary, sweet spouse, attentive, heareth, heareth and draweth to the couch, inly mourning as a widow bereft (what has he not been to her ?); kneeleth beside, attentive to comfort. The Son of Man heareth, draweth tenderly near, sitteth on the couch-side down, slideth an arm softly under, lifteth the failing form gently, draweth the head to His breast, closeth the other arm over, around. In Jesus' arms ! On Jesus' breast !

In the arms of Christ the Saviour
Softly dying, O, what favor !
Softly catching brighter gleams
Of the angel of his dreams ;
Painless parts the " silver cord,"
In the arms of Christ the Lord !
List the dearest, dying prayer :
' Lord, I yield her to Thy care,
Mary, cherished virgin wife,
Spouse and glory of my life ;
I commit her to Thy love
As I journey home above :
I the starry pathway take.
Cherish, Lord, yet for my sake !
Mary ! Jesus ! Sweet farewell !
I in heaven my love may tell.
I am ready ! Angels, ready ! '
And his happy eyes are steady,

And the rapt-breath fails to come;
Ready angels waft him home;
Blessed man, his work is done!
Blessed man, his crown is won!

The death-candle, it is lighted
In the cot on Nazareth hill:
Never burned death-taper, never bright as there;
Lo, an angel stands unseen, but standing,
Feeding slow the flame, murmuring as he feeds,
'Joseph!   Just Joseph!   Joseph the Just!

Asleep on the bier,
Hands folded gravely, eyes closèd deeply,
Long snow-beard drifting stilly over the breast,
    Over the winding-sheet;
Mary and Jesus kneeling there:
The light from the death-candle, lambent and soft,
Falling over the bier and its watchers,
Praying there till the dawn,
The angel still feeding the flame,
Murmuring the silent prayers between,
'Joseph!   Just Joseph!   Joseph the Just!'

The women of wailing come,
    Dismal and slow;

The funereal-women come with the dawn—
Locks dishevelled and torn, covered with ashes,
Garments of sackcloth and sorrow, trailing and rent—
Come, forgetting to weep,
A strange calm over faces distorted and weird.
The swallow twitters sweet from his nest 'neath the eaves,
The brown bees hum mid the flowers at the door,
And a honey-bird hovers over a vase of lilies at the head
of the bier;
Nature may sing when a saint journeys home.

BURIED.

O, grave of Joseph! Our hearts come to the spot. Sacredest tomb in the earth! If we may call it more sacred than Anna's, mother of the Virgin, grandmother of Jesus, or Joachim's, grandfather, and nearest man in lineage to the humanity of the Christ. Three sacred graves! The angels know the spot day and night. His night droppeth down. Mary cometh to weep at the grave.

(In sackcloth, close veiled, knelt by the tomb weeping.)

MARY.

Oh, spouse, God give thee rest! Oh, spouse, dearest, noblest, best, God give thee rest! Our fathers sleep here; our fathers will welcome: Joachim, the righteous; Anna, saint-mother, will welcome; and I shall to thee come, and sleep here. And Him?—Messias! Messias! We may not anticipate God, rather accept as He giveth; thus have I lived. But the spirits of the prophets look down to-night, Daniel, Isaiah and David. "His tomb shall be with the rich." "A sword!" The glory of Nazareth departeth! Numbered its days and few! Lord, God of Israel and David, thy hand-maid behold!

(*Jesus cometh to the grave to weep.*)

Jesus weeps at the grave of Joseph. Mary and Jesus weep at the grave.

EPITAPH.

Only man that ever lived intimately and long with Jesus on
    earth:

Only man that ever died in the human arms of the Saviour:

    Spouse of Mary, and foster-father of Jesus:

      "JOSEPH, A JUST MAN!"

CHAPTER IV.

BAPTISM-MORN.

I AM COME INTO MY GARDEN.—CANTICLES.

SCENE—*Vale of the Jordan.*

MORN, like a virgin rosy-lipped and fair,
    Sits on her Orient throne; forth from her fresh
And flowery robes delicious scentage goes;
From waving palm and white-thorn thicket comes
The melody of birds enthrilled with gush
Of gladness loosed. In the blue heights o'er head,

Cloud-drifts, with all their rich, warm coloring,
Roll gorgeously back; the red sun looks
With softened splendor down; rejoicingly
Each grass-spire lifts its green blade to the light:
'I live!' 'I live!' its soft sheen whispers low,
'In the great Father-smile I live and joy!'
Still-billowed Jordan grandly prestige-touched,
Swells to the verge where golden willows sweep,
And white-bloomed almonds flowery offerings cast
The healing wave where leprous Naaman seven times dipped.
Ho, waves! a greater than Elisha comes;
And populous Archelais sends her sons,
The people of Bethocan flock in crowds,
From fertile plains of Jezrabel they pour,
And all the neighboring regions wide about;
Up from the wilderness he comes, the Voice,
Clothed in the camel's hair, the man who eats
The honey from the rock, the locusts of the wood,
And day and night, the solitary wild within,
Lifts up for Israel th' solitary prayer;
Gaunt with the fast, man of the unshorn locks
And naked feet, like some old desert-rock
Half-mossed, the prophet of the border-land:
Up from the wilderness he comes and cries,
"*An axe at root of Judah's tree!*" "Repent!"
"*He comes!*"   "*The way of the Host High prepare!*"

Up from the wilderness he comes, and talks
Of one to follow yet, whose fan His hand
Is in, whose fire unquenchable shall burn.

The dense crowd-soul 'ware of God-presence grows ;
One draweth near, the foldings of whose robe
Float round with quietude of grace and awe,
Forth from whose eyes outbeameth the Divine ;
On through the hushed and parting multitude He comes ;
The hallowed air grows golden round His head,
And fragrant as a light wind fresh o'er beds
Of spices blown.

       (How that great prophet would
Have stayed the Christ and been at His pure hands
Instead baptized, all which th' sweet evangelists
Have wrote, yet yielded to His Lord, turn ye,
And read.)

       The twain the Jordan-path
Go down. Along the bank two shadows glide ;
One like an earth-shade darkens on the sward,
And *One*[1] the shinings of the sun exceeds.
O, Jordan-tide ! thou, too, baptism hast !
The brightening shadow of the Christ in-dips,
The mirror-wave-glow taketh calm and tone,

The azure of the cloud that o'er it stoops,
The rose-blush of the oleander flower
Whose bough o'erdroops, the rich transparence paints.
Back shrink the dazzled crowds; but *One* anear,
Mother of HIM, englorified in HIM,
The secret of the Heavens, the mystery
Of God on her illumèd brow outshines;
Her foot, soft and uncovered, holds the marge,
One hand the flowing veil draws trembling back,
And one close pressed unto her heart to stay
Joy-floodings full.   Th' dark Hebrew eyes wax large,
The color grows upon her cheek, her lips
Burn with high thought, but recollected hold
The revelation grand that waits to roll
From th' hearkening heavens low-bent, uplifted t'ward
In high solemnity the prophet-hand,
As all the multitude hold silence far:
The Jordan to their girdle drifts and calms,
The waves-baptismal consecrate the Lamb;
A DOVE from out the cloud! and lo!
Deep sounding through cerulean depths afar,
A voice from off the Throne, "MY SON BELOVED!"

> O glorified humanity baptized!
> O Christ, amid the brightened waves!

O Jordan shore—surrounded—lost, in the great grandeur of that voice, reverberating still from sky to sky, lifting thy bright palms up a-beat with sweet, irradiate bewilderment, as beats the heart, and every plume brightness-retouched, on the wide-spreading wings of him, the angel tall, who stands the Throne before, oft as God speaks.

O Mother of the Christ! amid the shining palms down on thy knees in silentness of rapture sunk! The sweet Magnificat and " My soul magnifies " rolls yet up from thy heart.

HEART OF MARY.

My soul is ravished with joy in God my Saviour! Thou hast owned Him before Israel! Thou hast made Him known unto Judah! His chariot-wheels tarry not! Messiah maketh haste! His kingdom shall be from everlasting to everlasting; "for He who is Mighty hath spoken." He stoopeth down over the Jordan! The waters saw and were glad! The Jordan saw and rejoiced! "What aileth ye, ye little hills, that ye are afraid? What aileth ye, ye mountains round about Jerusalem, that ye tremble? Father! Son! Holy Ghost! "Glory as it was in the beginning, *is now*, and ever shall be, world without end! *Gloria Patri, et Filio, et Spiritui Sancto!*"

O, FATHER speaking from the heavens that brightly bend
    above,

O, SON within the sacred waves, whose other name is love,

O, SPIRIT from the opened cloud, sweet melting, searching
    Dove,

        The TRIUNE-VISION bright unroll,

        And leave the picture on our soul!

CHAPTER V.

FORTY-DAYS DOLOR.

WHO IS HE THAT COMETH OUT OF THE WILDERNESS PERFUMED WITH MYRRH?—CANTICLES.

PART I.

SCENE—*Evening of the Baptism.*

THE mother at her lattice pensive sat,
  And for His coming watched.   He was not wont
To tarry thus.   Oh, chill and desolateness
Of a widowed home!   Now, He who 'd ever made
That poor abode, in joy, or woe, of Heaven
The very gate, was gone!   Gone, strangely gone!
Gone as the Christ mysterious!   She saw
Him from the wave, the desert-way go up,
But such a glory round the dripping robe,
But the marvellous Dove was on His breast,
And feared to follow her baptizèd Lord,
Drawn by the Spirit forth.

                    The midnight came.
The night had never at her casement sighed
As wild and dark.   Down on her knees she seeks relief

In prayer, and cannot pray.   Not pray !   She who
Has ever found an open door within
Unto the very cherubimic seat.   But 'stead,
A knowledge in her troubled soul that clouds
Are round about His head, and fiends, and snares,
And paralyzed and faint can only wait.
Mother of Sorrows, thou didst Him lose
But three days once, and thy heart well nigh broke ;
Now, forty nights must dismal trail o'er earth,
And forty mornings rise in beauty sad,
And thou canst only wait, and fast, and weep.

PART II.

Scene—*Fortieth twilight of the Temptation.*

Yet never swerve her eyes from loving watch.
> (*Christ appears winding up through the paths
> of distant fields.*)

Him yet afar she runs to meet.   She puts
Her arms His neck about, she kisses Him,
And, sunk down at His feet, her joy out-sobs.
Gaunt from the famine of the wilderness,
Yet all the Saviour breaking through His sad
And haggard face, the Christ above her bends
With that love in His look, instant the mother knows
Whatever now she asks may granted be.

9

The memories of all late agonies
Come over her afresh, she upward looks;
Those giving eyes shine in upon her heart
So sweet, faith wavers not.

MARY.

                              By all my hopes
And fears, and by the Sacred Babe I've borne
And fed from my own breast; by each rich joy
Of thirty garnered years, till it had seemed
I'd waited for this woe, this glory long,
Had not those years been each a cup from Heaven
Whose nectar overflowed, so let me share
Each coming triumph, or each nearing woe!
Give me when distant held, this grace, *to share!*

JESUS.

Woman, thou askest much, a very sword!
Knowest thou the sorrows that thy Son must bear?
Yet God shall give thee strength.   I grant it thee.

And Mary, blessèd, kissed her Christ-Son's feet
Content, and rose with haste to give Him bread,
For sore was He a-hungered with the desert-fast.

CHAPTER VI.

MARRIAGE OF CANA.

"AND THE MOTHER OF JESUS WAS THERE, AND BOTH JESUS WAS CALLED
AND HIS DISCIPLES."

PART I.

WHERE the sycamores tall their branches spread
   Over a fountain that laughs as it leaps in its silver bed,
      Where the green rush grows
      And the wild rose blows,
And the violets purple the dewy turf,
Fringing the lids of this beautiful eye [5] of the earth,
Where the guests are in robes, and the kid of the feast is
     spread,
Sit the happy parents of those who come to wed,
And the learnèd scribe with his learnèd scroll,
      In his hand the reed
      Ready for need,
To bind and to bless and to write the rite on his roll.

What's the joyful shout in the summer air?
The voice of the youths and damsels fair
      Who in circle-ring
      In baskets bring

From the sheaves of the reaper afar o'er the plain,
A tithe of the golden-bearded grain;
'Tis the chime of the timbrel-call on the distant green,
The answering note of the tambourine
        From the bridal-train
        Over the plain.
She cometh, the beautiful bride, in shining array,
In the tunic bright and the sandal gay;
        Like a crown inlaid,
        Each ebon braid,
The bloomiest buds of the rose-spray twine,
An' veil of silver lace o'er all, through which the blushes
        shine;
And he, the bridegroom, handsome, rich, and young,
The purple thalid o'er him flung;
        She draweth nigh
        With downcast eye
        Like maiden shy;
Over the bride, over the groom, flaunting its silken folds,
The flowery hupah[6] bright unrolls,
Over the twain that wait for marriage bands,
Over the parents that join the willing hands;
        " With this ring I wed,"
        Hath the bridegroom said,
And the nuptial wine hath the maid-bride lipped,
To its ruby depths hath the bridegroom sipped:

Their love-glass see
Dashed 'gainst the tree;[7]
And the bride-mother feeling her heart to glow
With the nuptial blessing she beareth to whisper low,
Drawing nigh
With a woman's sigh,
Over her beautiful daughter's trembling head
The thalid[8] of her wedded lord to spread—
Whose blushes now
In a charming glow
Burn to the brow,
As the fruitful grain[9] the merry matrons fling,
As the marriage canticle they sing.

And there falleth soft on the greensward bright,
Than sunshine fresh from the heavens more light,
To hallow their mirth,
Light not of the earth;
'Tis Jesus a guest, who to bless doth stand,
And touches the ring with holy hand.

PART II.

Over the plain and away in Olympic-like race,
The young men vie in the panting chase:
With eye like a star,
A maiden afar,

The racer he knows by a voice in his soul,
Gazes on him and the nearing goal,
                And a smile will seek
                The olive cheek
                Of that maiden meek,
And a warm glance shoot from those starry eyes,
As he lays at her beautiful feet the prize.

The damsels of Cana anon o'er the glade
Spring forth to the call in the nopal shade,
                To the psaltery's sound,
                Ranged gayly around,
As the tinkles ring out from the tambourine bells,
As the seven-reed flute of Tophim swells;
And the elders look on with a serious smile,
Or live over their own love-bridal the while.

                But the goldenest ray
                Rings the seventh day,
When the beautiful bays encircle each victor head,
And the crowning feast 'neath the tent is spread:
                Fresh fragrance showers
                From the gathered flowers,
And a deep joy broods o'er the festal hour,
For Jesus is there, and reigns with His sweet secret
        power.

Lo, the guests from heaven wind[10] down through the
     paths of the plain,
The guests unbidden, the stranger train;
Blandly they drink to the fair bride's beauty and health,
Blandly they quaff to the bridegroom sons and wealth,
       And the wine-tides grow
       In the goblet low,
And a paleness comes to the bridegroom's brow,
For shame that the wine-pledge faileth now;
But Mary is here, and Jesus her son:
True, never a miracle yet for man hath He done;
Yet blessedest mother doth askful say
('Tis for troubled friends ever her sweet lips sweetest
     pray):
       " Know, my Son, Divine,
       They have no wine ! "
       " But what can it be,
       Woman, unto thee,
       Or what unto me ?
Mine hour is not yet come," grave answers the Son;
But the mother hath asked, and she knoweth the asking
     won.
Nor more saith the Christ; but she, mother of Him,
Hearken, ye servants, His words : " Fill the urns to the
     brim."

Six urns at the door
The Christ bent o'er;
The crystal ripples took the shadow of His brow, and
flushed;
" The modest water saw its God, and blushed,"
Nectared to wine
By hand Divine.
Others drink their best wine in the first cups past,
But the givings of God grow sweet to the last.

CHAPTER VII.

THE MINISTRY.

MY VINEYARD, WHICH IS MINE, IS BEFORE ME.—CANTICLES.

THE unction stirs His lips upon, who taught
As never man.   Low at the Master's feet,
Disciples sit.   The hour has come.   What hopes
Ardent in that sweet human breast arise,
What shadowy certes of the grief to come;
Yet calmly kisses she his sacred cheek,
Watches, how more than motherly, His steps
Depart, and turns unto her daily task;
For she was poor.   She, in the sight of Heaven
The richest woman in the full earth, wrought

For her bread.   Think of this, all ye meek ones,
The crumbs of carefulness who eat, and wear
Of poverty the garb, God's chosen ones,
The rich in faith, are most-times poor.
Their legacy in Heaven's sure treasury
Falls not until they step from mortal shores
To the sweet everlasting.   And Jesus
Went forth unto His Father's work, and preached
That glorious sermon of the mount, when meek
Yet God-like on its brow He sat and taught,
In sweet beatitudes, the multitude.
She saw the palsied walk, the cripples leap,
The seventy sent forth to the ripened fields.
She saw

    The trembling matron in the press
    Was healed when she but touched His dress;
    The ruler's daughter, pale in death,
    Received again her sweet young breath;
    And Nain's widow o'er her dead
    The blessed tears of rapture shed;
    The leper lost his leprous skin;
    The sinner lost her shame and sin;
    Within the wilderness when led,
    The famished multitude are fed;
    Where'er He turns, the poor oppressed,
    The wretched everywhere are blessed;

9*

One only purchase-price, " Believe,"
And ye the priceless gift receive.

"The transcendent beauty of the three years' Ministry seemed to make it impossible for her to endure the Passion; and did it not seem to show, as if by the beauty of His preaching alone, and by His human tears, and His vigils on the mountains, and His foot-sore journeys, and His hunger, and His thirst, and sweet patience, and the persuasiveness of His miracles, and the wondrous enticing wisdom of His parables, the world might be redeemed, and Calvary spared ? "—FABER.

----+----

NOTES TO BOOK V.

1. SCENE from Faber's *Mary at the foot of the Cross*, also verse 2d, p. 175.

2. Joseph is last mentioned in the Scriptures returning from the feast of the Pasch, when Christ was twelve years old. From the text that He (Jesus) was subject to His parents and grew in years, it may be inferred that he lived during those years; and likewise it may be inferred that he was not living at the time of the marriage of Cana of Galilee, or the Evangelist would scarcely have particularized, "and the mother of Jesus was there, and both Jesus and his disciples were called," and omitted mention of Joseph, had he been present. And still more at the crucifixion, where Jesus bequeathes his mother to John, is her widowhood apparent. Epihamus says he died soon after he returned from this feast. (*Hares*, LXXVIII.) St. Jerome, a little before the baptism of our Lord. Cyprian and others think him to have been alive and present at the crucifixion. Gentillucis, in his *Life of the Blessed Virgin*, remarks: "It is probable that his death took place a little while before our Lord began to preach, because he was then spoken of as one recently alive: 'Is not this the son of Joseph?' And had he been alive at the time of the passion, our Lord would not have recommended His holy mother to John, but to the care

of her spouse." The Latin Church celebrates his death on the 19th of March, and the Greek on the 20th of July. Bede says, " He was buried in the valley of Josaphat, near the sepulchre of the holy Simeon."

3. God is truth, and light His shadow.—PLATO.

4. The gift of vision is an olden tradition. Abbé Gerbet adopts it in his *Lily of Israel,* supporting it with fair ingenuity of reasoning. He confers it however at a different time, and gives it a far different scope. For instance, he imagines the holy mother only witnesses the crucifixion through this gift, making it thus take away from the real rather than to superadd. The gift, as we represent it, is not greater than a prophetic vision; and looking into the present alone, it may indeed be regarded as not equal to the glance down where *free agency* works out *predestinate will.* Simple tradition, as far as we understand, merely attributes the gift without any special time of conferment.

5. The Hebrews call springs the eyes of the earth.

6. Literal copy of a Hebrew marriage contract: " In the year . . . the day . . . in the month of . . . (Benjamin) son of . . . has said to (Rachel) daughter of . . ., Become my spouse according to the law of Moses and of Israel. I promise to honor you, to provide for your support and maintenance, according to the custom of Hebrew husbands, who honor their wives, and support them as seems meet. I give first . . . , and promise you, together with support, clothes and other things necessary, conjugal love, a thing common to people of every nation. (Rachel) has consented to become the wife of (Benjamin), who, in order that the dowry should be proportionate to his means, willingly added to the sum before mentioned, the sum of . . . ."—*Mosaical Inst.*
Thus were Joseph and Mary married. Thus the bridegroom and bride of Cana.

7. Thalid, a mantle.

8. Hupah, a bridal canopy, borne by a group of youthful attendants.

9. The Hebrew bridegroom dashes the wine-glass to the earth as an emblem of the brittleness of all human joys and ties.

10. A part of the marriage ceremony was the casting of the grain,

brought in the baskets of attendants, by the matrons present, toward the bride, as they sang the marriage canticle.—GERBET.

To the same writer we are indebted for a description of the race and the dance, under the nopal shade.

11. The Orients call their unexpected visitors guests from heaven.

BOOK VI.

OR

BOOK OF THE PASSION

"AND A SWORD THROUGH THINE OWN SOUL!"

'Twas the hour when one in Sion
   Hung for love's sake on a cross,
When His brow was chill with dying,
   And His soul was faint with loss;
When His priestly blood dropped downward,
And His kingly eyes looked throneward.

MRS. BROWNING.

CONTENTS.

CHAPTER I.

"THE HOUR COMETH!"
I HAVE GATHERED MY MYRRH WITH MY SPICES.—CANTICLES.

SLOW creeps the purple eve round Olivet;
The full round moon looks softly down, the stars
Attracted hang its sacred brow above;
The olive trees beneath, in little groups
Of twos and threes, the dear disciples sit;
In openest view, lo! Peter, James, and John.

PETER.

In spirit and accord with holy law,
Have we not come up to the feast?   Think ye
The Jews will seek to stone us as of late?

JAMES.

Can crafty scribe, can subtle Sadducee
Plot 'gainst, and He not know?   Our Master reads,
Of men, the very heart and thoughts.

Judas Iscariot (*drawing stealthily near—aside*).

'Tis false! false as a vaunting wizard's boast.
My heart, He readeth not.   Doth He?   Ha! ha!
Wonders He worketh with a cunning will;
Yet were He mighty as He saith, and loved
As much, why, He the very waste might turn
For our grand pleasurement an Eden-land,
Ay, every desert-rock to gold a-gleam;
Forsooth, when that He doth, I'll worship too.
Praise on! praise louder on, ye favored three!
'Tis meet, 'tis just, the confidence who share;
Not I, beholding e'en that beardless John,
With voice as woman's in beseechings soft,
Preferred, loved more than all the manlier Twelve;
Now am I nerved to scoff.   Despised of men,
I weary of this bootless following:
Could He read hearts He might know me, perchance.
The Priests would give—— Hark! hark! "Beware!"
        Back! back!

(Bitten by self-sting in his jealous heart,
Recoiled like serpent of the poison fang,
In deeper shades nursing his own black thoughts;
Pursue him not; turn quick where shines the moon.)

Peter.

Son of God! and God.

JAMES.

                    God ?   I know, the Christ,
He is.

JOHN.

    And very God !

PETER.

                    His miracles
Are more than prophets work.   Devils, I heard
Proclaim Him thus, and knew.   Lo, He but speaks,
And straightway they leap forth, submitting dumb.

JAMES.

And John ?

JOHN.

    I looked into His blessed eyes.

PETER.

And saw such love ; for no man hath such love.

JAMES.

The Son of God, and yet of woman born ?

PETER.

O, there's a mystery, His birth, that shrouds,
All but my· high apostleship I'd give
To know.   I've seen (and my heart reverent grew)
Messiah's mother on Him look.

JAMES.

And this?

PETER.

Through centuries have Judah's daughters watched,
And for this honor longed.

JAMES.

And yet no pride
Sits on that brow serenely lit.

PETER.

At times,
Great times, still I have watched, and seen,
As when He to Jerusalem late rode,
A glorious triumph in the eye.

JOHN.

Ah, yes;
But, oftener such a sadness in their depths,
That I have turned away with tears.

JAMES.

Apart,
She with the Master sits to-night.

PETER.

Low bends
His head, as if in some high comforting;
I marvel much the words.

John.

Her hands enclasp !
Ah, me ! Woe, me ! if we the Master lose.

Peter.

Thou speakest, John, as though thou wottest not,
The earth hath promise of Messiah's reign.

The burning words of prophecy
A promise bright bestow,
Messiah's righteous reign of peace
An end may never know.

The Lion of brave Judah's race
Shall rise and fill His throne,
And strength and glory in His days
To Israel be known.

James.

Heed take ; again, we hear the Master say,
" My kingdom is not of this transient world ; "
And in His tarryings with us of late,
More than a mother's tenderness hath shone,
A growing sadness in His deep, fond eyes.

Peter.

Dear Christ ! Great Christ !

John.

Where He transfigured shone,
Moses, Elias, talked with Him of death;
Th' Prophet of th' prophets o'ershadowed draws
Into the cloud—and it is death!   O, Christ!

Peter.

Not unto death!   Dark are Messiah's words
For human eyes; yet is He not the Christ?
The everlasting Christ?   And can it be,
It be thou shrinkest first, thou lovingest
Of all?   I unto death will follow Him.

CHAPTER II.

PASCH-NIGHT.

"THE HOUR HAS COME."

PART I.

"Thy palmy groves inlaid with precious flowers."

THE home of Magdalene, a mansion fair,
   Whose sculptured walls arose amid the groves
That round it swept in beauty Eden-like,
Rose-laurels[1] where the nightingales thick nest,

And pride of statelier palms, and elegance
Of cypress shade and fir; "for she was rich,"
And beauty was a passion in her soul
As in her radiant face; fair Magdalene!
And to this day there's hamlet named for her,
Where the old crone at her rude door will sit
And tell how zealous Magdalene, forgiven,
Followed the footsteps of her Lord, and gave,
At length, all of her substance great, the poor.[2]

PART II.

" Soft be thy tones, my harp,
Like some autumnal breeze whose murmurings
With the deep notes of falling waters flow ;
Meet for sadder themes."

SCENE—*A chamber in the mansion ; a couch ; the wings of an
angel overspreading the couch.*

I SLEEP, BUT MY HEART WAKETH.—CANTICLES.

Oh, Pasch-night darker than in Egypt-land!
The sleeper tastes the supper with the Twelve,[3]
The mangled body in the broken bread,
The priestly blood of sacrifice that flows
The mournful cup within, and faintness creeps
Unto her heart; still in her sleep she prays
For calm, and only to abide with Him.
" I sleep, but my heart wakes:" on flows the night:

Out on the Galilean sea she looks,
White with the waves that shoreward rave.
Strange sight !   The moon, paler than erst her cheek,
Peers cautious from a sky in cloud.   Strange sight !
Th' Syrian nights for constant clearness of their skies,
For splendor of their stars are known ; now screened,
The moon walks timidly in veil, and sheds
Her light as waning prayers one path athwart,
Who walks, would he but read ! ' There's warning out ; '
A doom that reaches up with greedy arms,
Knells in the stealthy footfall ringing scared
Upon the pavement stone.   The frighted night
Hath whispered it unto her winds that surge
The doomèd city's naked streets ; and yet,
Oh, deaf ! the life-nursed passion-spell of hell
Coils round the jealous heart.   Oh, fiendish blind !
For lucre and for hate he madly dares
The path of horrors leading swiftly down,
The portals of the second death a-gape
And groaning for his coming loud ; and heaven
O'erspreads, nor can as yet together roll
And flee.   The Son of Man as it is of Him
Written goes.   Mother of Dolors ! aghast,
Thou canst not on such sad betrayal look.
A tear drops from the angel's eye who spreads
His white wing o'er thy bowèd head.

Oh, doleful night !   A-knocking at the door,
She hears the hour for which her Son
Was born into the world.

PART III.

"I ROSE UP TO OPEN TO MY BELOVED, AND MY HANDS DROPPED WITH MYRRH."

SCENE—*The Mother of the Betrayed upon the housetop.*

'Tis midnight mid the cypress boughs beneath,
'Tis midnight with the veilèd stars above,
And it is midnight in the heart of Mary :
Fixèd and cold she stands, the moon's pale sheen
Upon her brow and mournful hair unbound,
The sword-point at her heart, the shaft that ere
The morrow midnight pierced it through.   She was
Alone : alone in all the world she soon
Might be.   There was a tremor of the lip ;
But stars of bygone years re'lume,
And all their lingering brilliance shed
To shine this dark hour through the boding heart.
She feels her bright Babe's first soft breath afresh
Upon her cheek ; she lulls her fair, young Child,
The shadow of the pyramids beneath,
Kneels by the Jordan-wave, the wine-urn fills,
And sees the fever leave, the plague-spot stayed,

10

The crazed in right mind at a Saviour's feet,
And he to whom the world had been but dumb,
The voices in whose ears are sweet astonishments,
Wind-stirs in air, the water's bass, bird-song,
And best of all the music of his mother's lips,
Till, thrilled with the sweet mysteries of speech,
He finds his lips unloosed.   Dead Lazarus hears
His voice, shakes in the clinging cerements
Of the grave, and walks in his damp shroud out :
Yet, He must die !   And crippled to her knees
She sinks ;—(looking into Gethsemane ;)
Darkness and sleep born not of other night
Are there ; and sadly sorrow-worn,—'twas so
To be fulfilled ;—the dear disciples sleep,
Can ye not watch, O Peter, vigilant !
O John, beloved ! the one hour more ?   Yet there
Is one who weeps, yet watches from afar,
While He apart, the Man betrayèd, prays
Alone.   No, not alone ; with more than flesh
And blood He wrestles now, the human Christ ;
The hosts of hell come up unto the gates ;
The Tempter of the mount again returned [4]
Beside the agonizing wrestler stands,
Holds up the nearing horrors of the cross,
And questions if a God no way can find,
Nor other scheme a wretched race to save ?

The willing spirit groans, weak is the flesh,
In sore amaze, and hell's o'erwhelmings leave
" Exceeding sorrowful!" " Sad e'en t' death!"
In agony of prayer the scathed lips part,
" *The bitter cup, my Father, let pass by!* "
O, God in heaven! large drops roll off from Him,
And they are blood!   " *Father, Thy will be done.*"

Submitted Christ!   Sweet Son!   Yon sable cloud
In heaven rolls back, an angel passes through,
An angel o'er the yielded Sufferer bends,
And lifts the dewy locks, and wipes with touch
Like balm the bloody sweat, and raiseth up
The Son of Man they did betray, with wings
Of healing wraps Him tender round, and folds
Him to his heart till He is strong.   (Thus when
The cup comes to our lips, we yield : He sends
His angel down.)

            With staves, the Judas-band!
The Cedron brook is crossed!   Convulsively
To stand, her hands the fretted terrace clasp.
In vain!   The waves go over, and she sinks :
She who can only weep, as only she
May ever weep.   Oh, mother of the Man
In dark Gethsemane! the Man betrayed!
Poor tears we weep for thee, poor tears for Him,

Poor tears for our great sins bringing the woe.
Day-streaks are in the East: she sees them not;
The mother of the Man of Sorrows weeps.
Day-stirs are in the street: she hears them not;
She giveth all her tears.

       'To Pilate!' grows
The rabble-shout.   She wraps her vesture close,
And with a calm upon her saintly brow,
That sickly calm that with a crushed heart comes,
Goes from the house-top down.

CHAPTER III.

CONDEMNATION-MORN.

PART I.

Pilate was in the judgment-seat,
His guard of stern-browed Romans clustered round.

" The proud vicar of the despot sate,
While plumèd warriors stood in solemn state
Behind his golden chair."

JESUS was there, the growing majesty
   Of all earth's sorrows shadowed on that brow;
Yet tenderly around those mournful lips,
The yearnings of a pity nestled still

More deeply beautiful than saintliest smile
On lips all-glorified.   And jealous priests are there,
And multitudes like hungry locusts swarmed,
And clamorous for His blood who harbored ne'er
A thought unkind.   Down on the pinioned Christ,
Pilate, he looks, and dimly sees the God;
Red-eyed Robanni[5] like a tiger glares.

ROBANNI.

This prophet, false, is a seducer vile,
And stirreth a seditious populace:
And thou save him, Christ-king! God-Son! Suffered
A treasonous multitude to lead, not friend
Of Cæsar thou!   (Ah, rancid poison poured
Into ambitious ears!)   "All Galilee
He even now excited hath."

PILATE.

And wot
Not ye, that Herod ruleth Galilee?
Ye, zealous, law-abiding priests! hence bear
Your king!
(*Aside.*)

I'd not on one like Him in judgment sit!
Yet, Cæsar yet, and Herod! It is well!

PART II.

SCENE—*Claudia kneeling before Pilate.*

CLAUDIA.

My noble husband and my lord, have nought
With that just Man to do ; for Him, for thee,
How suffered I in dreams !   It was the hour
When spirits walk the earth and whisper free
Unto our souls, and draw them forth to see
Strange sights, husband, I saw this Jesus then ;
Upon a cloud of gold he sat ; above,
Around, beneath, angels with silver wings
Outspread, in worship mute—and He uprose ;
Yet even as I gazed, from other cloud
As night—(And Pilate stood beneath, his brow
Was pale ! his hands dripped blood !)—slowly and stern
Within a death-knell tolled ;· tolled three times three !
Which augury into my soul has burned,
Which knell tolls in my ear this day.   My lord,
Let not the blood of the Divine-Man shed,
Stain my sweet husband's hands.   Condemn Him not !

PILATE.

The gods forefend !   Away, kind Claudia,
A heel of iron rings without.   Thy prayer
Is good.

CLAUDIA.

And heard?

PILATE.

And heard!   In peace depart.

PART III.

SCENE—*Jesus returned to Pilate.*

The rabble grows,
The perjured witnesses press on, and Pilate strives,
Vainly, the waves of turbulence upon,
The oil of gentle words to cast.   Hisses
Are on the tongues that late hosannas sang.
Oh, it is swift in th' perverted heart
To be ungrateful and unstable strange!
But, I have heard from gray tradition's page,
And am inclined unto the old belief,
When Judas did his blessed Lord betray,
With mad joy flew the gates infernal wide,
And hell upheaved till o'er the darkened face
Of the whole earth all reckless passions swarmed,
And brooded like a legion vast, and men
Whose hearts before had human been, straightway,
Perversely dark with love of evil grew,
And thirsty for the blood of innocence.

ROBANNI.

Treason ! to government and Rome !

CROWDS.

Treason
To government and Rome !   Treason ! treason !

The cheek of Pilate blanching with each shout,
God, man, the fear, wavering betwixt—
The growing tumult-rage, alas ! to stay,
Too weak ! the guiltless Christ is sentenced to—
Expectancy's short hush, breaks as the slow
And self-smote sentence faltering falls—" *the scourge !* "
And disaffection's murmur, like the wave
Unto the rock that cast it off, returned
In swollen might, heaves in the distant crowds,
Rolled in its growing wrath back to his teeth.
Unhappy judge !   His angel good hath flown.

PILATE.

With Him,
And what ? your Christ, your king !

CROWDS.

BLOOD !   BLOOD !

PILATE.

" His blood
Upon your hands ! "

CROWDS.

" His blood upon our heads !
His blood our children's heads upon ! "

Oh, curse,
That shall to after generations cling !
She who had washed her Saviour's feet in tears
Faints in the hall, the tender John enclasps
A pillar in the court to stand, Peter,
With mingled grief and fear, astonied shakes,
Mild Arimathea for a pardon sues,
And wary Nicodemus, sudden grown
Bold as the murderous mob, indignant calls
For law and justice from impartial Rome ;
But Pilate stands, turned fixedly aside
From that meek thorn-wreathed brow, with glance
That dares not meet those calm, sad, prisoner-eyes,
Or scan the pallid face of her who stands
Widowed and child-reft there, as hearing not,
And writes the direful condemnation out.

10*

CHAPTER IV.

VIA DOLOROSA.

SCENE—*In vision, from afar.*

'WHAT seest thou, oh, my soul?'

A scourging-post!—hands unresisting bound
Unto the ignominious ring! shoulders
Without a blemish fair bared for the thong!
A victim, self-surrendered, silent, pure,
Suffering the malison of sin unmoved!

'What seest thou?'

     Crimsoned lashes in air!
Hearing the heavy scourge descend, hearing
The knotted braids bed in the quivering flesh,
A mother not afar, and fainted not:
O, blessedness of love! love that outlives
The prosperous hour, and casts out fear and shame,
And stands by brigh'tning in the trial time;
O, blessed love!

  'The scourge-post round! What, soul?'

Delirious wretches, furious that they wring
No groans from lips with th' stinging anguish white,

Impatient for the tortures of the cross!
Hands purpled with the tightened cord, unbound!
A mangled body 'neath a heavy cross!
A blessed Saviour with derision dragged
Through streets where He had golden precepts taught,
And healed their sick!   Earth growing hellish fast!
Gored shoulders bent beneath the painful load!
A darkness creeping o'er the dizzied eyes!
The robe of purple rent, dust-stained, blood-stiff,
Clinging unto the lacerated limbs!
The sinking sufferer fainting on the ground!

'Oh, soul!'

        A woman with a shriek that chills
Unto the Scourged, the Fainted, fearless sprang,
Rude soldiery, mindful they a mother have,
A mob ferocious stayed, a mother there,
Uplifting to her lap the swooning head,
While deathly horror creeps along each vein
And curdles cold around the stricken heart,
With coming strength that she has wrestled for,
Locking each bursting sob within her breast,
To bear with Him the crushing sorrow come,
Rending her veil the bleeding wounds to stanch,
Wiping with her soft cheek the bloodied dust
From off the smitten brow, laying her lips

With tenderest kiss where every thorn hath pierced,
Calling upon His name sublimely calm.
Slowly the Saviour's piteous eyes unclose,
Meeting the mother-gaze; two human hearts
With a high sympathy met in the waves
Of woe, enclasped and strengthened each its load
To bear! Love-tenderness as beautiful as death
Is grim and void and cold!

                              ' What seest thou? '

The cross removed, the cross upon one laid
Whom Jesus loves, meek Simon of Cyrene
Submitting patient to the shame.   O, man,
Bearing thy bleeding Saviour's cross, O, man,
Favored and honored this day more than kings!
The angels they will point thee out in heaven
A thousand years from now, and say, ' Behold,
This is the man who when the Saviour fainted
Bore for him the cross up Calvary ! '

CHAPTER V.

CRUCIFIXION.

"AND WHEN THEY HAD COME TO THE PLACE WHICH IS CALLED CALVARY, THEY CRUCIFIED HIM."

"Stabat juxta crucem Jesu mater ejus."

"O, ALL YE THAT PASS BY THE WAY, ATTEND AND SEE IF THERE BE ANY SORROW LIKE UNTO MY SORROW!"

WE have come unto the Mount, my heart faints!
God-tragedy! what words have I to paint
Christ-groans, Christ-wounds, man-jeers, hate, love, death,
    life—
All passions to their culmination rose
That beat in heaven or stir the breast of hell?
How can I tell of Calvary?'   The scaffold
And the axe a-grim, distinguished horror take,
That stand out on the calendar of blood:
A human butchery upon we look
And sicken at the sight; but awful life
As awful death, in awful poise the heart
That holds, is here—and I the pain would grasp,
The glimmer of the God instead I catch;
And I beside in speech am impotent;

When every line should run with pulses thick
As words, and each bleed like a gaping wound,
There is in them no *pain*, no *fire*, no *blood!*
Oh, Mount of sorrow and of myrrh!
Oh, spotless Victim shining! Bleeding God!
I give it o'er.   But stay, I see a woman here,
And my soul clambers up the cliffs to her.
Golgotha * trembles with the surge of souls
That 'gainst its fastness of rock hard press ;
Like sullen soundings from a storm-lashed sea
The fiendish roar follows my footsteps up
The grim " Place of the Skull."   In its eclipse
Of pain that face I know.   Beside her, stand
I may, and tell of Christ and Calvary.

Behold the Man condemned stripped for the cross,
Lots for the garment cast his mother wove,
And but a cloth, already blood-besprent,
Girt round the loins.   There is a moment's rest :
Such rest as waiting for the instruments of death,
The hammer and the spikes in sight.
Grim lictors stretch their victim to the cross,
His tender lips sweet-breathing still, " *Forgive!*
Father, forgive! "   The murderous hammer falls,
Drowning that sweetest prayer that struggled e'er
To rise. Oh, God! and are these men ? Has earth

No human left ?   *There is a mother here.*
Each cruel blow that breaks those soft, sweet hands,
And teareth through that tender corded foot,
Crushes her heart.   'Twere nought to die ; yet, no,
Bore she not the God-Babe for this ?   No love
Is deep that bringeth not forth pain ! *pain !* PAIN !
Corroding shadow to all love of earth !
Oh, mother, standing in the dire eclipse !
Speechless !—moveless !—transfixed in woe !—each crash
Thy heart counts with a spasm and a chill !
Was ever human love and woe like this ?
Yet in the light of His the Lovingest,
A ray absorbed.

                    Look up to the Divine,
'The bloodied rood is earthed !   With garments dyed,
He who from Bozrah comes and treads alone
The wine-press of our sin, is there ; behold !

' I cannot look, the shadow of His cross
Falls on my head !   Upon the battle-ground
Of heaven and hell, I palsied stand ! '

                    Look up
To *Him*, He dies for thee ! the Martyr-King !
Like victim of the murderous Indian's hate,

Naked and honeyed o'er, and pinioned hung
In Southern woods swarmed o'er with deadliest stings,
All crimes of men clustered his soul about,
All leprous shames of earth, the heart of sacrifice
Like plague-spots eat; each tortured vein
With anguish t' a purpled roundness swollen,
Each sinew shrunk and tightened with the pain
That in its clutching fingers grapples fast
The wildly-palpitating heart, and snaps
Singly and slow each shuddering string, and bears
Down on the writhing brain its iron palm;
And yet, crushed in the wine-press dire, those eyes
All-seeing, search the wilderness of woes;
The veilèd God-Being goeth silent up
The frowning mountains of our sin, the cliffs
Of a rebellion mad, scaling with pained
Yet onward foot the rocks precipitous
Of pride, ambition's giddy precipice,
And patient down the passion-gorges deep
Of man's despairing guilt, along the wilds
Of griefs untracked, the shoreless lake of plagues;
The knotted cords upon that brow stand out,
The terribleness of calm, smote majesty
On that meek forehead greatened grows, bloodied
And pale, lifting with the strained loftiness
Of painèd Deity. Oh, life! God-life!

Oh, suffering God! Oh, undiminished Christ!
Insatiate murderers on his death-pangs gloat,
And yet, no execration mars those lips,
That pant in stillest agonies apart.
Dear Christ! His hand is nailed unto the wood
But Justice, inexorable, eternal,
Holds to His lips the cup that could not pass.
Dear Christ! He drinks the curse! He drains the wrath
God-sustained, bearing th' world-woe to redeem.

The crosses they are three. The Incarnate
Dieth in the midst of thieves. The tallest
And th' centre cross is His. "*King of the Jews!*"
Glares on the mocking parchment o'er His head.
And one there crucified, even while death
And the grim horrors of the charnel-house
Widen the death-ring round his groaning lips,
To see the Christ in calm, bearing like pain
Of iron-wounds with anguish glorified,
Fans every fiendish passion of his soul.
Poor wretch! cross-scoffer with the Jew! In sight
Of world-salvation lost! Lost with such blood
Sprinkled so near! Baffling His great travail for thy soul!
Dying with Jesus! Going from His side
Down to hell! Oh, Christ! and in thy agony
Hearing the tramp of those who follow him.

Rejected Christ! to lose one soul!   One soul?
It is the trampling of a multitude
Whose feet are shuffling on the stairs of death!
Oh, Christ! seeing the darkened host go down!
Through all the coming ages going, going down!
And must it be, forever be, to drink
The cup, to clasp the dole, to die and lose?

Twain are the thieves, but one his eyes uplift
To see the priestly blood drop slowly down,
Each crimson drop illumed.   The memory
Of other leprosy, ah, not so black!
Comes over him afresh.   He softly weeps.

(Voice from the cross of the thief.)

"*Remember me!*"   O, miracle of love!
That will in every corner of the earth
Be told round dying beds, illuminating
His sweet uttermosts, the Christ, swift-saving
As a God, in His great pardon opening
Such window into heaven, "THIS DAY WITH ME
IN PARADISE!" he, the Penitent Thief
Of the cross, hangs in the sudden glory
Of the view with shine upon his face.

"Three are the crucified!"   I see but *One*:
Afresh the blood gush from the gaping wounds

Torn wider by th' weight of th' writhing form
Hung up betwixt the earth and heaven.   The rood
Creaks with His growing pang.   My God !   The air
Grows horrified.   The south wind call answers not
To th' north.   " The hills he toucheth and they smoke."
Dumb earth wraps in the shadow of His woe,
With travail of the smothered God-groan heaves.[9]
Mother-woman !   Oh, moment of eclipse
And earthquake in thy soul !   Close to the last !
Lo, others grovel on the quaking earth ;
Thou, every sense grown seven-fold acute,
Hearing strange sighs in the troubled airs ; thou,
Seeing Calvary with angel wings o'erspread,
Seraph-brows down cast, tears in immortal eyes,
And Gabriel by—the wings of mightiness
Low-drooped—hearing unkennelled demons howl,
Knowing hell is unloosed, and yet one cross,
On its huge wooden arms high up, dearer
By every pang (what most we suffer for
That most we love), one Crucified casting
Its shadow o'er thy sight ; and thou, standing
In the strange darkness silent, tearful up,
Taking that one cross in, great as the sea
Thy broken-heartedness ! all ye that pass
Attend and see if there be sorrow like !
" *Stabat juxta crucem Jesu Mater !* "

Hours three, dreadful and long, darkness prevails,
That crucifix transfigured on the glooms.
Like half-extinguished star unsphered, the lids
Of inner Deity uplift, baffling
The dole. In blood the garment rolled and laid
Aside! the uttermost, the gap 'twixt God,
'Twixt man, in naked agony wedged 'tween!
"Human, bleeding feet," standing in the footprints
Of our sin! Wrapped in the curse! The hosts
Of seraphim took wing! The Upper Throne
In cloud! Jehovah-Father, great! appear
For Him! "Darkness and clouds are round about,
And darkness He hath His pavilion made."
Alone! the God-forsaken One, to bleed!
To die! Our curse, our sin, our shame hung up
The goblet of malignest ill alone
To drain! "Thy water-spouts go over Him;
Deep calleth unto deep; the floods come up!"
The cold, *cold* sickliness of man's despair
When the lost soul finds the sweet heavens shut,
The gates of blessedness forever barred,
Comes over Him, of all God's creatures now
The most forlorn.

       Voice from the Cross.

    Eloi! Eloi!

Lama sabachthani? *My God! my God!*
Why hast Thou me forsaken?

The Deity

Off-shut! hanging and groaning like a man!
God! Father-God! if Thou apart must stand,
The human leave a mother yet! Thou hast.
The groaning of His lips she hears and knows
That He is there.

"ELOI!" "ELOI!"

Hell leaps! The stars are stricken in their course;
But, movèd by His lamentation loud,
Th' eclipsèd sun bursts out and crimsonly
And slow the creaking crucifix unveils.
He looketh down, the Christ, sweet Sufferer!
The pain upon His mother's face He sees,
Love stronger than the writhing pang illumes
His bruisèd eyes.

["His eye was now resting upon her. . . . His eye was resting upon the same object on which it rested the moment He was born, when He suddenly lay upon a fold of her robe upon the ground while she knelt in prayer, and when He smiled and lifted up His little hands to be taken up into her arms, and folded to her bosom. . . . . She looked up into His face. Never did two faces look into each other and speak such unutterable love."] [10]

Voice from the Cross.

WOMAN, THY SON! BEHOLD!

Heart of Mary.

Son, I behold!

Voice from the Cross.

THY MOTHER, JOHN!

         (Sweet scene!
Thus the Disciple of the Cross receives
The Master's only earthly legacy—
Sublimest tenderness!—John weeps.)

Voice from the Cross.
I THIRST!

The sponge of gall unto the gasping lip:
Again the numbing deathly shiverings;
The drainèd veins creep up.

Voice from the Cross.
IT IS FINISHED!

The hour is sped, the direfulness of sin,
Of death the bitterness, the cross o'ercome.

(*Two angels glimmer down and hover over the cross-top.*)
First Angel.
On that white face a sudden shine!   Those lips
Illume.

Second Angel.
God-life, coming like victor forth
Rejoicing for the guerdon won.

Voice from the Cross.
FATHER,
THY HANDS INTO MY SPIRIT I COMMEND!

And heavily the clammy breast upon,
That maimèd head in the cold victories
Of death awfully God-like still bows down.
God's Lamb is slain.

CHAPTER VI.

BURIAL.

SCENE—*Joseph of Arimathea and Nicodemus going up Calvary
with spices and fine linen.*

UNTO the crosses come, in sorrow standing,
Gone all the conscience-smitten multitude,
All save the sullen guard, who as a leech
On some scarce breathless corse insatiate clings,
Thrusts barbarously the clay-cold side within,
The wanton spear.   The rich flood follows close ;
The fountain flows on Calvary !   Oh, blade,
Stained with His blood ! Oh, piercèd, bleeding Dead !
Painful to Arimathea's tender eyes,
And in the righteous ruler's movèd sight,
Oh, flagrant shame upon the Sacred Slain !

NICODEMUS (*to the Guards*).
And will ye mar the Dead that Pilate gives ?

The guilty spearman shrinks: left are the twain.
Gently, as though that breathless body were
An infant child alive to every touch,
The spikes from the extended hands are drawn
And in their arms the mangled form received;
Weeping, the crown of thorns removed
From off the brow of death, and tender washed
Each bleeding bruise, the stark, wound-stiffened hands
And feet with ointment and fresh balm up-bound.

(Nicodemus and Arimathea anointing and preparing the body for burial.)

ARIMATHEA.

" I will the third day rise," and, He hath said.

NICODEMUS.

The third day [10] will the ransomed spirit rise
And find in Abram's blessed bosom rest.

ARIMATHEA.

If not the third, until, His great ghost may
Be hovering near, or standing white beside,
Unseen, but here.

NICODEMUS.

It may.

Arimathea.

If so, O, man,
Most marvellous ! He knoweth that we love
Him still.

Nicodemus.

He knows !

Arimathea.

And present, thus repeats
Unto my heart, " I will the third day rise " !
He that hath others raised——

Nicodemus.

Impossible !
This broken body live, were miracle
Outshining all such lost world ever saw.

Arimathea.

I have Jairus' angel daughter seen :
O, she was lovely ere she died, as breath
Of flowers, but lovelier in her second life,
And walks as though in heaven her father's courts :
She might believe——

Nicodemus.

Look on this piercèd heart !
These mangled limbs upon, so faultless fair
In moulded whiteness once ! Oh, never was

11

There mortal man so beautiful ! so good !
And yet so marred !   See, albeit blood-drops thick
Lie in this goldenly-brownèd beard,
The beauty rich of each full wave.

Arimathea.

         What glorious Man !
Of whom the prophet-psalmist chants, " And grace
Was poured His lips into."

Nicodemus.

         And most His eyes,
His glorious eyes !   When those grave lips began
With some high thought to warm, 'twas great to look
Up into them.   I came, ah ! well I mind
The midnight hour, the words of prophecy
To weigh.   This Jesus looked on me, and straight
I felt my heart transparent grow, His eyes
Beneath.   E'er since that glance my memory haunts,
And ever echoing in my ears still rings
" Thou must again be born " !   Yet, this *is* death !
Oh, shame upon the envious scribes who wrought !
Oh, lasting shame on coward Pilate's name !
Oh, woe to thee, Jerusalem, the lost !

Arimathea.

Ay, heard we not this Prophet say,

As sadly up this road of death He toiled,
" Weep, women, for yourselves, and not for me " ?

NICODEMUS.

Verily ! and my soul so indignant grows
At this mad flux of sin, I almost can
An amen put !

ARIMATHEA.

But prayed He not " Forgive " ?
And with His dying breath ?   Oh, He was e'er
The Merciful !

NICODEMUS.

The deeper shame on all !
And darker the desert of those who could
The Man of Mercy slay !

ARIMATHEA.

He waits the grave.

NICODEMUS.

Where shall we lay Him now ?   Impiety
It were polluted grave to give, when He
With Zion's kings entombed should sleep.

ARIMATHEA.

I have a garden nigh, within, a tomb
Hewn newly from the rock, a grave in which

Man never yet hath lain.   I thought to have
Within it with my children slept, but now
I give it unto Him.

Nicodemus.

I would I had

A tomb!   Unto this sepulchre the earth
In pilgrimage shall come.

The exalted Dead

Is shrouded for the burial, and that
By loving hands.   The kingliest of earth
Had never such caressing touch, tender
And pitiful as a young mother's hand
On her dead babe; such tears and such regrets
As those for Him thus slain, He whom they loved
And looked for Israel's redemption from;
For when " on Him they looked whom they had pierced,"
The Roman spear the last stern prophecy
Fulfilled, nor earth, nor hell had power to lay
A hand irreverent on the holy clay.
Slowly and sadly the Reverenced Dead is borne
The stately sepulchre unto, and laid
Within the grave-niche down, and tears like rain,
Of those who laid Him there, sprinkle afresh
The sheaf of balmiest spices on His breast.

Over against the sealed sepulchral stone,
Cleophas' wife and Mary Magdalene sit down
To weep!   The Roman guard is at his post.

CHAPTER VII.

IN THE TOMB.

"SEALED IN THE STONE-COLD TOMB."

PART I.

ALL the night is sad and moonless,
　　All the morn is drear and tuneless,
Not a birdling's warbled note
On the dolorous airs afloat;
All the pulse from earth is fled,
Nature mourns her Maker dead.

Awe and gloom earth-bosom shroud,
Void and silence sky-brow cloud;
E'en the hearts of men are chill,
Doubt and dread all bosoms fill;
Man-Divine, but breathless clay,
All earth-beauty fades away.

Yet, while heathen sentry round
Pace the consecrated ground,

There's a watch of longing eyes
Gazing wistful from the skies,
Guardian eyes of seraph-light
Bigger grown with wonder bright.

In a cloud two angels stand,
Starry fingers linked in hand ;
Not an angel's breath is heard,
Not a silver wing is stirred,
In their robes of light and bloom
Bending o'er that Sacred Tomb.

PART II.

SCENE—*Cottage of John—Saturday night.*

Where the sad disciples meet
Trace with me their muffled feet :
Low and mournful is each tone,
All their hope hath strangely flown :
Hearts of love are sorely tried,
Since the Master, He hath died :
Never sadder day did rise,
In the tomb the Saviour lies.

Thomas has barred the closèd door,
   The Eleven sit down to weep ;
For love of Him, their buried Lord,
   A solemn fast to keep.

Here James, he wears a sackcloth robe
    And mourns a kinsman dead,[11]
And the funereal ashes lie
    On weeping Andrew's head.

The robe of Jude is rudely rent
    With bitter grief in twain;
And deep the sons of Zebedee
    Lament their Master slain.

Bartholomew's high brow of thought
    With inward grief is pale,
And Simeon with a stricken heart
    Takes up the funeral wail.

Philip with faint and fearful breath
    Bows low his troubled head,
And mournful Matthew muses on
    Israel's Messiah dead.

E'en ardent Peter's kindling eye
    Is dim with gathering tears,
E'en to his bold and hopeful heart,
    No ray of light appears.

Now droops his head like some proud bird
Whose wing the tempest-cloud hath stirred,
Like eagle that hath soared too high
And crossed the lightning in the sky.

Ah ! how he mourns denial now,
Repentance shadows on that brow,
It mirrors in that swollen eye,
It deepens in that heart-heaved sigh.

PART III.

" O cor amoris cur conversum es in globum doloris? " *

SCENE—*A chamber in the cottage.*

Turn we to this chamber lowly ;
Ponder !   Here is grief that's holy :
The Mother of the Crucified,
In death-like swound e'er since He died ;
Within the cold, sepulchral gloom
Her heart lies buried in his tomb.

PART IV.

That twilight Judah's sabbath grew
A waning day of deathly hue,
That evening hour two sabbaths met
That midnight Judah's sabbath set.

---

* *O, heart of love, why art thou changed into a globe of sorrow?*

NOTES TO BOOK VI.

1. MAGDALENE, "a very rich, young Jewess of illustrious descent, her chateau situated among the rose-laurels which border the beautiful sea of Galilee."

2. Bayard Taylor's *Syria and Palestine*.

3. We have not adopted what some believe, that the Blessed Virgin partook of the last supper with our Saviour in Jerusalem; but we can imagine with Blosius, "that, filled with the Holy Ghost, she saw in spirit the outrages suffered during that horrible night;" in spirit this most sympathetic daughter of the prophets shared the closing Pasch and first Eucharist.

4. And the devil left Him *for a little season*.   Luke iv.

5. Several times during the past ten years a curious document, purporting to be a copy of the death-warrant of Jesus Christ, from the archives of some old library, has reappeared in various journals of the day, in which the accusations against Jesus are entered, with the names of his chief accusers, among the latter of which were two brothers, the Robanni.

6. One of the most ancient and tender of the Christian traditions. The paragraph where the Mother meets her cross-laden Saviour-Son, as He sinks fainting to the earth, is a scene drawn from the *Lily of Israel*, already several times credited for traditions.

7. The Jews have a tradition that the grave of Adam was on this Mount; also, "Augustine and others believe that upon this mountain took place the sacrifice of Isaac, figure of Christ."

8. A slightly elevated mount, north and west of Jerusalem. "Tertullian, Bede, Augustine, Jerome, &c., believe Golgotha to be in the centre of the globe. "He hath wrought salvation in the midst of the earth." Ps. lxxiii. 12.

9. Pliny and Strabo mention the earthquake felt even in Italy. St. Dionysius, the Areopagite, who was an eyewitness of this eclipse, thus describes it: "We were both standing at Heliopolis, looking,

11*

when unexpectedly the moon came before the sun: nor was it the time of the conjunction, and yet there it remained on the sun's disc from the ninth hour to evening."—*Epist.* 9. Moved at so strange a sight, the Areopagite exclaimed, "Either the God of Nature suffers now, or the fabric of the universe totters." Cornelius a Lapide adds, *Comment. in Matt.* xxvii. 23, on the authority of the ancient historians, that the Athenians, by the advice of Dionysius, raised an altar to the UNKNOWN GOD, from which St. Paul took his text to preach Christ. Origen, *Tr.* 35 *in Matt.*, relates that Phlegonthes, a freedman of the emperor Adrian, an exact chronologist, stated in his writings that on that occasion the stars were seen in the heavens. " *Quarto autem anno* 202 *Olympiadis defectio solis est facta ; dies hora sexta, ita in tenebrosam noctem versus ut stellæ et cælo visæ sunt.*" Origen, Lyranus, and Maldonado think this darkness only covered Judea. It was the general opinion of the Fathers, however, that it spread over the whole earth. Eusebius and Tertullian say that the Romans inscribed this phenomenon in their annals as an extraordinary thing, and the testimony of Dionysius confirms it; for how could he have seen the eclipse at Heliopolis, if it had not been universal?—GENTILLUCI.

10. A paragraph from Faber's *Mary at the Foot of the Cross.*

11. The Jews believed that the spirit did not ascend to its rest in Paradise till the third day after demise.

12. James " the brother of our Lord," and James the son of Zebedee, are often mentioned by the Evangelists. Mary, wife of Cleophas, was the mother of the apostle James, known as the brother of our Lord. (*Am. Ency.*) According to which we should reckon him cousin. The Jews reckoned as brothers the sons of a father's brother, where there were no true brothers, or again the nearest of kin. Some writers have also supposed that Joseph had children by a former marriage; though this latter opinion is strongly opposed by the Latin doctors. The suggestion that Jesus was other than the only son of Mary, seems at best reflective and unharmonious. Mary once spouse of the Holy Ghost and mother of the Divine Saviour, a virgin-mother sanctified unto Heaven forevermore, is the one voice of the Latin and Greek Churches, and concurrent belief of some able Protestant critics.

BOOK VII.

OR

BOOK OF THE GLORIES.

"QUEEN of Empires, in the tomb
    Buried must thy glories lie?
    .   .   .   .

Lowly Maid, around thy throne
    Ever swells the angelic hymn;
Hear us, where thy starry crown
    Lights the home of seraphim."

CONTENTS.

CHAPTER I.

RESURRECTION-MORN.

> " Lo, the gates of death are broken,
>   And the strong man armed is spoiled
>   Of his armor which he trusted—
>   .   .   .   .
>   Vanquished is the Prince of Hell ;
>   Smitten by the Cross, he fell."
>
>   " Smile praises, O sky !
>   Soft breathe them, O air !"
>   " Sing, sing, for He liveth !
>   He lives as He said !"

SCENE—*Garden of Gethsemene, near the break of the day—Servius
and Quintillus, guards, before the tomb.*

SERVIUS.

(*Timorously drawn backward from the tomb, in listening attitude.*)

THIS tomb within, my ear bodes stir ! *sure stir !*

QUINTILLUS.

A ghostly fancy overwrought ! the chill
That cometh with the dawn.   Morn streaks the east,
Look up !

SERVIUS.

It is the morn ! the third since which—

Quintillus.

Didst ever know a dead man from his grave
Out-walk ?   Arouse thee, man !   Such phantasies
Off-shake !

Servius.

        Like shrouds to dead men's bones they cling ;
I cannot shake them off.   One Lazarus
I've heard He raised, and three days dead.

Quintillus.

The same

Is it a *dead* man and a *live* to be ?
What then ?   Methinks thou art demented come,
· And for a soldier and a Roman fast !

Servius.

We saw him die !

Quintillus.

We did !   Gods do not die !

Servius.

Upon the battle-eve, when the scared moon
Pale stood the ghastly slain above, we've stood—

Quintillus.

I've stood by Servius a soldier then, be not
A croaking raven here.   I hark no *stirs*.

(*Vision.*)

Quintillus pacing, and sturdily,
His beat.   Servius drawn silently a-back,
Eyes grown to the sepulchral rock.

(*Prayer.*)

Clear, Lord,
Let Thou the vision rise!

(*Vision.*)

Palm-grot indistinct,
Door and rock wading in glooms, over the Tomb,
Waded half in the sepulchral damps,
Steadily o'erbent, their gloom-repelling brows,
The angels two.

Heart of Servius.

Elsewhere I have known no glooms!
Elsewhere I have known no tombs!
This, *this* is *the* tomb!
This, *this* is gloom!
This, *this* is fear!
Watching here!

SCENE—*Angels of the Watch—Angels of the Ministration—The Angel of Miracles—The Angel of Rewards.   Which may have been
supposed to have attended the ministry of our Saviour, to have
gone with the seventy sent forth.   The one working the cure,
and the other conferring the grace following the cure. Lighting*

ANGEL.

Well thou might, for all the night
Were thine eyes anointed quite,
Thou a sight more dread might see
Under yonder cypress tree ;
Sight that almost freezes me.
Lo ! there sits a Rider pale
Darkly clad in deathly mail,
On his horse so strangely white,
Rearèd in his stricken fright,
Reinèd by the Rider's might
On his ghostly haunches back.
Seest thou that bloody track,
And the hoof with crimson shod
From the field of carnage trod,
From the battle's gory sod,
Lifted in the hushèd air,
Held in frighted terror there ?
And the shadowy, lifted mane,
The fiery eye glared o'er the plain,
And the champed and frothy rein ?
Scents that pale steed sore defeat,
Doth he fear the shock to meet ?

SECOND ANGEL.

Closer, closer, hold our breath !
Know that Rider's name is Death.

ANGEL.

Who defeat hath never known,
Fatal have his arrows flown,
Earth with dead and dying strewn.
He has watched his keen darts hurtle
Through the shade of rose and myrtle,
He has mocked the bride's despair,
He has scorned the orphan's prayer,
He has won the brave and fair,
In the flush of youth and health,
In the strength of years and wealth,
He has joyed to see their fall ;
In the beggar's lowly stall,
In the noble's bannered hall,
In the dungeon's lowest cell,
Aimèd sure, his shafts have fell.
Dreaded foe in mortal bower,
He has snapped the fairest flower ;
On the scorching desert-sand,
Round the ocean breakers' strand
Tyrant king in every land,
Doth that dreaded conqueror feel
Fear around his heart-strings steal ?

SECOND ANGEL.

Hold !—The doleful damps illume !
Darkening through his gathered gloom,
Darkening on the bright'ning Tomb,
Are his deadliest glances sent !
Hold ! his deadliest bow is bent !

SERVIUS.

                    It shakes !

LOOK ! LOOK !

        And Servius stood with livid cheek
And pointed hand as rock-cliff rigid
In the air, and hardy old Quintillus shook ;
For sounds the sepulchre of rock within,
Like to an earthquake grew, and as one dead
With Servius fell ; for one whose brow was like
Unto the lightning for its flame, came down
And rolled back the stone and thereon sat
As on a throne.

ANGELS OF THE WATCH.

He cometh forth the Risen !
Ho ! thou, who the pale horse ridest, bow down
And pass more reverent on to fulfil !
Into His kingdom there shall come no Death.

PART II.

Scene—*Entering at the gates of the garden, Magdalene and Salome, and other pious women.*

In silent wonderment they come, feeling
The earth beneath their timid footsteps throb ;
Bearing an offering of spices sweet ;
The night scarce flown, the trees in shadow lie,
Taking unto themselves dim ghostly forms
As the pale women hurry tim'rous past.
Unto the trembling turf, what roots the foot?
A robe of white over the rock a-drift :
The angel of the Resurrection-Morn
The glory of his eyes upon them lifts.

ANGEL.

The Crucified ye seek.   He is not here.
Look in and see.

MAGDALENE.

> (*Women within the tomb.*)
> Lo, He hath gone ! the Lord !

(Each other's faces into, sore perplexed,
Greatly in awe, they look, and turn.)

ANGEL.

> (*Sitting upon the right hand of the tomb-vault.*)
>   The Christ
From the dark chambers of the dead hath walked !

Second Angel (*beside*).

Go, and the sad disciples tell.

They come
With shine on robe and brow—the risen watch
Astonièd see, and venture furtive glance
And flee.

PART III.

(*Peter and John have been descried by Magdalene walking in the garden ; have stood by and looked into the vacant tomb, John believing, Peter doubting ; have departed " seeking the brethren ;" Magdalene watching their retreating footsteps ; the doubts of Peter clouding.*)

But, no, she cannot go,
And turns to the deserted tomb again.
The very spot where He hath lain is dear.
(*Looking down into the tomb.*)
Fresh tenderness o'er her sad spirit comes ;
Like one in some invisioned sleep she weeps.

(*Angels sitting in the grave-niche, one at the head and one at the foot.*)

Angels.

Why weepest thou ?

O, angels, question not,
Ye who have never known a clinging doubt.

There is no stir without: in Mary's heart,
Speaks the presentiment, 'Some one is nigh!'
Nor rising from the tomb down by whose door
In tears she kneels, she turns.   Her risen Lord
Behind her stands.   'Knows she not Him, the Christ?'
Her eyes are holden at His will, we read:
But ours are loosed.   We vision had but now
That lingering floods: th' Christ in His new glory
Looking down into that upturned face
In its sweet sorrow lost, holding the power
When He has gathered that forever precious grief,
To deluge it with joy.

JESUS

" Mary !"

MAGDALENE.

" Rabboni !"

(In bright o'erwhelmings lost, her hand outstretched
For clasping of His robe.)

JESUS.

" Forbear to touch !"

One moment crowded with ecstatic joys,
Her loosed eyes drinking risen glories in,
And then with holden sight again alone

She stands ; but with the morning in her heart.
O, it is morning in Gethsemane !
O, it is morning over all the earth !
And this was morn full blown. ' Mornings ?' Mornings
Are beautiful in every clime.   The poles they touch
And every peak glows like a rose.   Yet not
Th' Orient ripest with sun-crimsoned hills,
The Orient's luscious summer never bore
A day so fair, so full, overflowing
All " the God-create," goldenly, tenderly ;
Nor sunshine fallen since that other morn
The brown earth's pillars first uprose and stood,
And all God's sons together sang for joy,
So pure.   O, morning resurrectionized !
She stands ; her quickened ear all glad sounds thrill,
Not wonted murmurings of growing things
The poet hears, sprouting of tender roots,
And bursting of young buds in fruitful-bosomed earth,
But the large joy warming the heart of Nature,
Giving pulse to the veins long grown a-cold,
Depth to her skies and verdure to her fields,
And best of all a pardon to her lord.

PART IV.

' Till by weeping Mary seen,
Where had He, the Risen, been ?

Walking in Gethsemane?'
Nay, it is a mystery sealed,
Never it hath been revealed;
  Yet a thought is drifted me,
Like a whisper strayed from heaven,
  When, that, Jesus conqueror rose
  Victor over tombly foes,
When the deathly shroud was riven,
First, He went up Calvary;
There beneath the crimsoned rood,
First in risen glory stood
Where He self had abnegated
Till a fiendish mob was sated,
Where His sufferings bought a world,
  And the Adam-curse redrest.
How His lighted God-eyes fix
On that frowning crucifix
Where His body fainted, moaned,
When the justice-bolt was hurled,
  Fiery bolt against His breast,
Till the creaking cross did shake,
(And man said, 'The earth doth quake,')
As the God-strength undiminished
Struggled till the price was finished.

O, earth-conquerors, bow ye down
At the brightness of that crown:
  12

What are all your triumphs worth,
Triumphs stained with guilt and shame,
Feeble victories of the earth?
Mundane grandeurs, how ye fail,
How your sickly honors pale,
Glory sunk to nothingness
In the light of that uplifted brow,
In the blessing of that name,
Who for fallen man hath travailed,
Who in dying hath prevailed!
Pardon's cup of blessedness
Piercèd hand is holding now!
And another chord is added
To the ringing harps above,
And a higher strain is chanted
For the pardon newly born.
Glory! glory, crowns the morn!
King of triumphs! God of love!
Daysman 'twixt the shining Throne,
Sinner's Friend and Shield alone!

PART V.

Where went the Holy when from Magdalene?
Was it to stand the Thronèd bright before,
The clasping of the Infinite to meet,
Upon the bosom of the Father, glad

To lean a-down and cry, " I have travailed!
I have travailed and prevailed!   Piercèd hands
Behold! and give me back the glory erst
I shared."

                    Nay, with a tenderness as fresh
As when He was a child at Nazareth,
He tarries even yet, kind Christ, for one.
She comes, a deeper knowledge looking out
From those calm mother-eyes, pale from the swound,
And holier light on the madonna brow.
The glory of the morn that touched her soon
As e'er the shroud He burst, she who was fair
As day before, yet beautified it left
Her still.   Expectant in her heart she comes.
Nigh to the garden-walls the women wait,
Who joyfully to the disciples bore
The tidings of a risen Lord, and met
Such doubts their own poor faith had staggered back,
And like in vision follow silently:
Up through a shady lane they go: Jesus,
The Risen, in garments brightly beautiful,
Beneath the palm trees walks: He draws a-near!
The radiant, risen Son!   Mother of Joy!
Holding his shining feet enclasped, holding!
Rapt Magdalene had worshipped and adored,

But thou givest unto those feet nail-scarred,
Yet shedding light, thy kisses and thy tears,
Thou feelest the God-smile on thy bowèd head;
He who on earth had never smiled is not
The Man of Sorrows now; salvation sealed,
The first fair resurrection fruit He stands,
The life-eternal sparkle in each vein,
Each fresh pulse fed with life, love, glory, full!
Unextinguishable—full!   The smile o'erflows:
She looketh up, up through her shining tears,
Up to the Christ: the same loved features there,
The Babe of Bethlehem, the Nazareth-Boy,
The Man of Miracles, the Crucified!
Th' same save in th' bloom immortal now.
O blessedest of mothers! thy Son
Has died and rose again.   Arisen, God!

CHAPTER II.

RESURRECTION-EVE.

I FOUND HIM WHOM MY SOUL LOVETH: I HELD HIM, AND WOULD NOT LET
HIM GO.—SOLOMON.

THE day with morn of mystical glory
   In its fragrant airs, and noon of visions,
And eve with the disciples gathered close,

Rehearsing visions told, and Jesus looking in,
The day, each hour a very link of gold
For ages of this world and the next, had gone
Rich glory-laden down, and tranquil night,
Bearing her blessing of soft sleep, had come
To all. Not quite! If I of that may chant
Which like white-thoughted angel-whisperings comes,
Free as beat of the streamlet's silver pulse
Nigh to the sanctuary's sacred bounds,
Free as the lark-song at the gate of heaven
When morning goldens earth, if free? I sing
Mindful the heavens hear. 'And man!' What then?
My reckoning higher lies, and but with Him
Who willeth me to sing and fills my soul
With sweet thoughts till it overflows.

(SCENE—*Midnight; house of John; the sacred Mother.*)

She has into the depths of grief been down
And come too gloriously up of late
For sleep so soon; His first smile lingers still
In every chamber of her soul, and lights
Too brightly up each cloister where sleep
Would creep and spread his tranquillizing wing:
Pondering the glories of the morn she feels
Him near, draws back the curtain of her couch,
And Jesus in the moonlight stands revealed.

Mary.

Draw nearer, dearest Lord, draw very near!
　　(Jesus drawing to the couch-side near, standing beside.)
May I not come!

Jesus.

　　The Little Flock have need;
When I am gone, how will they to thee cling,
And thou wilt spread thy mantle over them:
Lovest thou me, fold my lambs.

　　　　[O'ermelted
As incense in a censer almost burned,
Consumed well nigh for love, His hand she holds;
As mother, more, yearning toward the dear lambs,
What will life be to her like without Him?]

Jesus.

Woman, let not your dear heart troubled be,
For thou art of the household of the Lord,
And but unto the Father's House, I go.

[And blessingly as Christ lays piercèd hand
On that dear head;—sleep cometh sweet;
His peace He left with her.]

CHAPTER III.

ASCENSION-MORN.

LIFT UP YOUR HEADS, O YE GATES; AND BE YE LIFT UP, YE EVER-
LASTING DOORS; AND THE KING OF GLORY SHALL COME IN.—DAVID.

ON Olivet the Anointed stands,
  And lifts to heaven His piercèd hands:
How can eyes that never saw
Paint the glory and the awe?
How can reverent spirit, wary,
How can lips that are but clayey
Sing unless an altar coal
Lights the vision of the soul?
There, He stands, the Glorified:
All His robe of spirit-whiteness
Downward flowing in its brightness,
Downward to a wounded foot
Making by one foot-track,[2]
Pressed upon the verdant sod,
Last on earth He ever trod,
Footstep of a parting God,
Making all the mountain holy;
  Golden girdle bright
Crossing o'er a bosom heaving
With the pathos of the leaving.

There He stands, the Crucified :
Soft glory trembles in the curls
That sweep the shoulders half-a-down,
Locks that late dishevelled hung
’Gainst a blood-red cross a-back,
All their floating roundness now
In a golden ether glow.

There He stands, the Sacrificed :
Light from the God-brow glitters down
On each pale olive tree,
And shinings lie on every leaf
That ’s witnessed oft a Saviour’s grief,
Till all the mount in brightness glows,
    As if to azure heaven
    Another sun were given,
    And all its dazzlings poured
    On Olivet’s fair brow.

There He stands, the Deified :
Yet His eyes how tender beaming,
So that mortal eyes can gaze,
Nor be blinded by the rays—
Eyes with all the knowledge gleaming
Sadly drawn from human life,
With the deep tomb-mystery

Gathered in the deathly strife;
Eloquent with glories heavenly
Never yet to earth revealed;
Melting with the grace-fount love,
That His dying hath unsealed;
Brightest eyes on earth that's been,
Sweetest eyes on earth e'er seen.

Five are His wounds and sanctified,
Sighing ever of one cross-tree,
Where He plucked the thistle-root,
Gave His blood our wounds to bathe,
Crossed for us the dark-gulf wave;
Emblems of His dying throes,
Tenderest proofs of Christly love,
How each blessed crimson scar
Gleams on hand and foot afar,
Brighter than a golden star.

Hush! He speaks, Omnipotence!
All ye fanning winds keep silence!
Passion-tossed and throbbing soul,
Every wayward beat control.
Those hallowed lips drop gospel-pearls,
Happy the ear those accents charm,
E'er while His solemn charge He gave,
His promise high to shield—to save,

12*

Now His voice in lofty calm
Rises in a last address,
" Little flock " to farewell bless.

Holiest benediction given,
From the lighted zenith lowered,
Lo, a cloud of amber near,
　　　　Downward floating—
Every radiant fold,
Softly burning gold—
Till the Christ upon it stands ;
　　　　Upward sailing,
Till from off its shining threshold,
Jesus soars up into heaven.
All the mount is people-thronged,
Thronged with wondering, wistful people,
Gazing up with eyes expectant :
Very near the brightened sky,
Angels, two, are standing by.

Mary, mother of the Ascending, apart for a space upon the brow of the mountain, under a clump of the olive trees, looking steadfastly up; heaven-way opened; a gleam of the city with gates eternal; Jesus ascending; Mary, face like an angel, looking steadfastly up.

MARY.

" Lift up your heads, ye everlasting gates,
The King of Glory at your entrance waits !

ANGEL (*at the gate*).

" Who is the King of Glory ? "

MARY.

The Atoner strong and mighty,
The Lord of Hosts, the Christ that died,
The Anointed, Risen, Crucified,
The Lamb of Calvary !

ANGEL (*at the gate*).

Lift up your heads, ye everlasting gates,
The Peace-Prince at your portals waits !

CHOIR OF ANGELS (*within*).

Ye heavenly gates, wide open swing,
Receive your walls within, the Glory-King !

CHAPTER IV.

MATTHIAS.

ACTS i.

GONE had the Christ, gone gloriously up
  The ransomed mercy-seat to take, nor more
To walk in guise of man the verdant earth
Made verdanter where His pure footsteps tracked
    Till the golden time await
    When the kid and tiger mate;
    Till the lion with the lamb lies down,
    Till Immanuel takes His crown,
    And the throned Messiah reigns
    Over all the conquered plains;
Yet precious in the Intercessor's sight
The little church left in a world of night.

SCENE—*An upper chamber, the Apostles of the Church, Mary,
Mother of our Lord, holy women, holy men, praying for the
Paraclete.*

And as they prayed, came to the quickened mind,
" His bishopric let thou another take."
Chosen were two, men sober and devout,
Of good deeds full, and great praise in the church,

'Twixt whom they could not choose, but mindful well,
God knows and answers every prayer of faith,
Provided they lots for the twain and prayed;
And thus for highest office one was chosen,
That ever man on earth was called to fill;
Apostle of the Christ, and to Matthia fell
The lot.   Mary the favored, prayed for him.

CHAPTER V.

PENTECOST.

" Dum lucis hora tertia,
　Repente mundis intonat,
　Orantibus Apostolis
　Deum venire annuntiat." [4]

CONSTANT in prayer that knows not wavering,
　　Still looked the whole church up and asked of God:
Peter, the zealous, stood up and preached.   Hearts
Late murderous with sharp remorse grew pricked,
Till sudden blown from shores of Paradise
Great winds the massive building shook,
And all the pressing multitude, down-smote,
A pardon sued.   The bright air pregnant grew
With tongues of flame.   Heaven's windows oped,
The Holy Ghost outpoured—and Mary saw
Three thousand souls converted in a day.

CHAPTER VI.

CHRISTMAS ANNIVERSARY.

WE WILL REMEMBER THY LOVE.—CANTICLES.

BRIGHT the midnight stars are blinking,
As they blinked a night of yore,
Tender, mourning mother linking,
This night with a night before.

Night she caught the air of fanning
Flung from raptured seraph-wing,
As her bright Babe's features scanning,
Heard the lays the angels sing.

Sacred mother, deeply sharing
Since that night the joy, the woe,
Cross of Jesus beauteous bearing
While she tarries yet below.

At this hour life's scenes come moaning
Through the holy midnight calm,
Scenes whose hours were dipped in groaning,
Scenes for which earth held no balm.

Now the wondrous mission pondering,
  Deeds that light and mercy shed,
Meekly with an outcast wandering
  One not where to lay His head.

Now a crucifix uprising,
  Paling all her eye and cheek,
Love and woe, cross and crucifying
  Never human lips can speak.

But an unseen hand is wiping
  Softly all her tears away,
And a shadow round her bright'ning
  Whispers, 'I am by alway.'

Till a light her brow is wreathing,
  Heavenly halo newly given,
And her raptured lips are breathing,
  ''Tis the first birth-night in heaven.'

ASSUMPTION - MORN.[4]

"WHO IS THIS THAT GOETH UP AS A PILLAR OF SMOKE, OF AROMATICAL
SPICES."

" A lily newly blown,
Radiant in stainless robes of lucent white,
Blooms in eternal beauty in the light
That floats around God's throne."

Immortality,
Name next in glory unto God ! that writes
Upon the gate of death 'Highway of Life,'
Whose shimmering whisperings sweetly fall as song-notes
Dropped from the lips of young immortal Hope,
O'erleaned the jasper walls to gaze a-down
Upon a Christ-bought world, an anchor-fluke
Down to the deepest thought-wells sounding cast,
An arrow to the heights of being sent,
A priestess rapt, heaping the heart-shrine high
With all the jewels of a holy faith,
Immortality, in all-gathered glow
Of spirit-glories draped, soft, nears thy feet.

SCENE—*Isle of Patmos—Hut of John, built like a fisherman's cot—
Dying chamber of the Virgin, John and Magdalene kneeling by
the couch.*

There's other light this sacred chamber in
Than moonbeams pale, cloud-like and still, a-float

Around the bowèd head of Magdalene,
Touching with gleams the robe of kneeling John,
And over her entranced who ardent waits,
Soft, starry floatings thickening goldenly
Until the sleeper spiritually still
And softly dying as the summer's rose,
Of love the beautiful traditions tell,
Lies in the light embossed.
                    Oh, exiled John,
Sweet son, the bright star of thy island home
Is setting now.   How in the eves to come
Wilt thou its hallowed beamings miss.   Sad are
Those bowèd brows; for unto loving hearts
Earth's sweetest friendships they are very sweet;
Yet no wail comes to jar the spirit calm,
An hour so bright they may not stain with tears.
The languid night creeps tranquil on; the stars
Stand at the midnight watch, the same high watch
As that bright night of yore, as lo! He came!
From the rekindling eye the dim mist lifts,
The waxen cheek with spirit-beauty lights,
A smile seraphic curves the brightened lip,
And wistfully the watchers' heads are low
And mute to catch the Dying's faintest breath.

Mary.

The death-sleep o'er me came but now,
    Or some deep spirit-charm:
I walked the shadowy valley-land,
    Nor felt one brief alarm;
For Gabriel held my hand enclasped
    Within his strengthening palm,
Of Heaven he spake and Christ so sweet,
    I lost the awe in blissful calm,
As over across the mystic Jordan
We passed, my Angel-guide and I,
Nor broke the ripple of a wave,
And walked that other earth—the kingdom of the Fathers.

Bending o'er one flower that met me,
Said my Angel, 'Heavenly Rose of Sharon,'
As I saw and drank the fragrance
Lent by Him who breathed upon it when He made,
Said my Angel, 'God made the roses all up here,
Sends His angels down to paint them,
And they do it very fair.'
And I answered, very—
Beauteous, tender flowers of earth!
Yet one budding of this rose is worth them all.
And the Eden grasses! and the Eden lilies!
    O, the verdure of the turf,
    And the whiteness of the flowerings!

Of such emerald brightness burning
  Never earthly foliage grows ;
Of such snowy whiteness fragrant
  Never clayey lily blows.
O, the glory of the gardens
Circling as the rings of Saturn,
Luminous and bright,
Round the House of Many Mansions !
Flowers rich as Asian jewels
Pictured in the velvet mosses,
Grouped in thrones and rainbow-arches,
Some in stars and some in crosses,
  Miracles by prophets done,
  Miracles of Christ the Son,
All the deeds the good have wrought,
  Every gentle charity,
  Every sweet humility,
Every saintly conquest won
Far down on the mortal shores,
There the Canaan shrubs and flowers
With their bright perennial leaves,
With their never-fading wreaths,
In a tableau fair in-wrought,
Burning moie than tints of even.

'Neath the majesty of trees,
Swayèd in the upper breeze,

In a heavenly wood,
In the forest round the garden,
All entranced I stood,
When I met, lo! that other beauteous mother,
She who dwelt in Eden's bowers
And pulled the new world's first young flowers,
She who plucked the fatal fruit
Whence all human ills first shoot,
She who lost her Eden queendom,
Purity and right of Heaven,
In one fatal hour
Yielding to the Tempter's power,
Lured man from Eden-home,
Doomed herself and all her race,
Till the Blessed purchased grace;
She who 'd washed her soul in tears
In her chastened earthly years,
She who 'd cleansed her heart in blood
Dripping down the Calvary rood,[5]
She it was, in rapt accord,
Came to greet the mother of her Lord,
Clasped me in her radiant arms,
Blessed me in the words of Eden.
'Lo! her seed had crushed the head
Of the serpent in our stead;'
From the chambers of the Fathers

Adam [6] went up with the Christ,
With the blessed risen Christ,
To the higher Heaven
Adam went in with the Christ:
In the garden of the Fathers
Eve was waiting still for me;
And we went up higher,
Mid the patriarchs in white;
On the Mount of Saints,
Where blest Joachim sits;
Anna-Mother life-encrowned;
And just Joseph from a throne
Beckoned me to come;
Scarce whose glorious brows I saw—
Lo, the deeper Heavens unroll—but no,
The glories of His PARADISE
No mortal heart may know:
But that glimpse of Jesus given,
Man on earth, but God in Heaven,
How it floods me yet afar,
You will know when you go
Where the Triune splendors glow,
Standing in the glory of the Lord with face uncovered.

Still sweet watchers,
Walking mid the glorified;

It was only earnest given
That I joy to leave with you,
That you grieve not sore when I go
Where they wait—Anna, Joseph, Jesus;
And I knew I had not died,
And I heard you still up there
Praying for a last adieu.

Gentle friends, again I've wakened
    To this ebbing life below;
Yet there waiteth one beside me,
    'Tis my angel guide I know.
Though his wings on earth are dimmer,
    Less the brightness round his brow,
Less through eyes that yet are earthy,
    Still he smileth on me now:
Smiles to hear me talk of Heaven,
Smiles to wait and waits to waft me!
O, the valley, it is pleasant!
With His rod and staff, with His angel,
It is pleasant going through;
Heaven coming down to meet you,
Till you scarce can bide to wait!
Yet I turn me once again, as the dying alway may,
    Glancing through each life-day
    Ere the last one counts for God.

Fair the groves of Palestine,
Sweet the Hill of Frankincense—
Nazareth rises to my vision !

There have been threads of gold
    In this life-web almost spun ;
There have been sands like diamonds
    In this glass I've almost run ;
But the gold-threads have been shadowed,
And the diamonds dimmed with sorrow ;
I joy that where there comes not change,
    I waken with the morrow ;
But most I joy in this bright hour, all, all have been for God.

Blessings on ye, gentle watchers,
    For the favors I have known ;
He will shower His blessings on ye
    For the loving kindness shown.
Blessings on God's holy church ;
    Like the goodly cedar tree,
Like the Indian forest banyan,
    I its spreading branches see
Reaching out from shore to shore,
    All the isles unto it given,
Till beneath the cross-tree kneeling
    All the nations under heaven.

When the shadows deathly creep
O'er mine eyes in silence deep;
When the funeral boughs ye reap,
When the tombly mound ye heap,
Ye, this loving watch who keep,
Say ye soft, and cease to weep,
" He giveth His Beloved sleep." '

As the starry lamps were dimming,
Sweet they heard the angels hymning;
Heavenlier grew the lifted eye,
And the rapt breath fainter came,
As the music rollèd nigher;
Earth upon the senses palled
That saw the city, light-in-walled,
And the pearly gates ajar
Far above the morning star,
Saw at Glory's shining gate
Christ the Son and Saviour wait;
And when morning crownèd earth
Woke to an immortal birth,
She went up with angels.

As the sunrise-gate was swinging
On its golden hinges wide,
Mary-Mother
Passed that other
Opened for the glorified,

Through the parting cherubim,
Through the gleaming seraphim,
Through the Thrones and Powers,
Banners lowered and crowns offcast—
Through the multitude no man may count,
Through the four and twenty elders,
Singing rapt their alleluiahs,
Round high Heaven's incensed altar—
Crossed the jasper floor of Heaven,
Nigh unto the rainbowed Throne,
All her shining face, growing shining
Every step she nears.

Wears the snowy robe of angels,
And the martyr's starry sandals,
Holy Mother's queenly crown ;
In the flood of beatific vision,
Leans on Jesus' breast a-down.

" And the Spirit said unto me, Write.   And I said,
What shall I write ? "

" BLESSED ART THOU AMONG WOMEN."

13

NOTES TO BOOK VII.

1. In the chapter upon the Resurrection, every vision mentioned in each Gospel has been introduced, and in the only way we could find so as not to have some one seemingly contradict some other one. We are aware that Dodridge and others have written at length on this point so generally assailed by the infidel, but have never yet read any of the dissertations endeavoring to harmonize the same.

2. There is said to be in a rock upon the summit of the Mount of Olives, the print of a human foot, which has the tradition that it was the last track of Christ upon the earth.

3.   " When as the apostles knelt
               At the third hour in prayer,
               A sudden rushing sound proclaimed
               The God of Glory near."

4. The 15th of August tradition commemorates as the day of Mary's death. "Nicephorus says, at the age of sixty-one years; Hypolytus, sixty-six, and Eusebius, sixty-eight years." There are also "various opinions as to the age of our Divine Redeemer at the time of His death. Some say thirty years, others forty (*Chrysost. in Joan.*), or even fifty (*Irenæus*, lib. ii.; *Hæres*, c. cxxix.). The most common opinion is, that He was thirty-three, or entering his thirty-fourth year."—GENTILLUCI.

5. There are several legends of Adam and Eve appearing at the crucifixion. One represents them accompanied by angels and bathing in a drop of the blood to remove the stain of the fall.

6. See BOOK OF NICODEMUS and early traditional records.

THE END.